TEMPLE OF SHADOW
BOOK 1
(AN ALBRIGHT ADVENTURE)

PHILLIP TOMASSO

SEVERED PRESS
HOBART TASMANIA

BLOODY FOOTPRINTS AROUND THE CAMPFIRE

<u>Novels</u>

Mind Play
Tenth House
Third Ring
Johnny Blade
Adverse Impact
The Molech Prophecy (as Thomas Phillips)
Convicted
Pigeon Drop
Pulse of Evil
Vaccination
Evacuation
Preservation
Sounds of Silence
Treasure Island: A Zombie Novella
Damn the Dead (Forthcoming from Severed Press)
Treasure Island: A Zombie Novella
Blood River
Wizard's Rise
Wizard's War
Queens of Osiris
Assassin's Promise
Absolute Zero
Extinction (Novella)
Jay Walker: The Case of the Missing Action Figure
Jay Walker: The Case of the Impractical Prankster
You Choose
Woman in the Woods
Before the Sun Sets

This one is, as always, for my kids
Phillip, Stephanie, Grant, Abby, Raeleigh & Anthony
And for my grandkids Vinny & Arabella
It is also for the dogs in my life
Ziti, Fettuccine, Cannoli, and Vader
I LOVE All Of You So Much!

PART ONE

Every man's life ends the same way. It is only the details of how he lived and how he died that distinguish one man from another.

Ernest Hemingway

1

Brazil - February - Twenty-five years ago

Travel during the middle of the heavy rain season was more dangerous than any other time of year. By all rights, the Koatinemo region was on par with reaching an average of eight inches of rain per month since December. It felt as if the region should be completely submerged underwater. Rain poured down from the dense, saturated rainforest canopy like a series of waterfalls. The overgrown vegetation spilled the accumulation, creating a series of dangerously swift, and sometimes deep, impromptu creeks. In drier areas, under the foliage, there was thick, gooey mud.

The Xingu River snaked through Brazil, flowing north toward the Amazon River, and passed between twenty-two million acres of virgin rainforest. The body of water was protected by the indigenous Kayapo people, who call the river *Butire*. Less than ten thousand Kayapo are spread throughout the Brazilian rainforest.

Alexander felt his skin wrinkle, his toes pruning. His army green floppy visor bucket hat, with a drawstring under the chin, kept the rain off his head. The blue waterproof parka kept the rain off his torso. The insistent downpour splashed against his neck and rolled down his back and into the waistband of his pants. His undergarments were soaked by rain and sweat. His chafed thighs made him wince with discomfort after every step taken.

He, his team, and two guides had been cutting a path through dense jungle for hours. If they'd managed more than a few miles, he'd have been surprised. At this pace, it would be days before they reached the treasure, if there was even a treasure to be found.

The lead guide, a former military man, stopped and held up a fist. They loved their hand signals. The guide had given everyone a crash course while on the boat. The most important hand signal was held up first. It meant stop and shut up. There were seven in his party, nine with the two guides. They all walked in a line, stepping where the person in front of them stepped.

"What is it?" Alexander asked. His eyes darted about. He only saw green. Giant fat tree leaves, and green ground cover. The jungle was one giant camouflage portrait. Every direction looked identical. Getting turned around and winding up lost would be easy. There was no clear path, other than the one they cut as they moved forward. When Alexander looked behind, he could not see much of a path. He looked for signs of machete bites in the wood, and slices through giant green leaves. Could the vines and weeds and branches have grown back already?

The jungle seemed alive, as if an entity. The canopy made it feel like eternal darkness below, during the storm. It was midday. It looked more like midnight. He knew by nightfall the forest would be black, unnavigable. If they didn't find a clearing, they would make camp beneath the giant trees. It was far from ideal, as predators came out at night.

"We're not alone," the guide whispered. He unshouldered a rifle, pointing the barrel toward the dense forest, and then opened the action, pulling the bolt handle up and back. He dropped ammunition into the magazine, slid the bolt handle forward and down, locking the cartridge into place.

Not alone? Alexander shifted his weight, regripping his hold on the machete. All of the thoughts that flitted through his mind during the hike were pushed aside. His body went rigid. The beat of his heart and heavy breathing drowned out the sound of rain falling. The sound was cloudy, muffled. He no longer heard the jungle around him at all.

A branch snapped. Alexander could not tell where the crunch came from. In front of them? From behind? He wasn't sure. "What was that?"

The guide *shushed* him with the silent gesture, a finger against his lips.

Alexander often found himself in predicaments, it came with explorations into unpopulated territories. The surge of adrenaline racing through his body gave him a high. There was no denying danger created an unparalleled rush. Part of him craved the reaction like a junkie, despite the unpredictability of the outcome. Living on the edge had become his way of life.

Something about this situation felt different, more sinister. What changed everything was Pricilla. They got engaged two months ago. A wedding was in the works. When it was just him, he didn't worry about his mortality. If he died out here in the jungle, she would kill him. She had told him as much at the airport last week when they hugged and kissed goodbye. He promised her he would return. He had no intention of breaking that promise.

One member of his team had had his first child, right before they left for the Amazon. It was all the man talked about on the plane across continents.

Alexander wanted a family one day, as well. It was why getting home safely was so important. "What do we do?"

"Keep moving forward," the guide said. His eyes scanned the canopy, and narrowed as he attempted to peer through the trees. The man needed a shave. They all did. "I don't think we're in any real danger."

Alexander looked at the rifle, the guide's finger on the trigger. He nodded at the weapon in the guide's hands. "You *look* like we're actually in real danger."

"We're good. We're safe," he said. The guide dismissed him, starting forward. The group followed. Alexander shook his head, then fell in line.

Another branch snapped.

They all stopped. They didn't need the guide to make and raise a fist. Not this time. Something was out there. Following them. Stalking them.

"Hey," Alexander said. Again he was *shushed*. The butt of the rifle was nestled against the guide's shoulder. He held the barrel in the hand of his extended left arm.

The man pointed with the end of the rifle barrel. "Came from over there. The last sound came from that direction."

"What's that mean?"

"Same as before. We're not alone," he said. The guide never stopped looking all around. "I'm just thinking. At this point, we're closer to the boat than we are to the X on your map. We're only a day into the hike. It makes far more sense to head back to the boat. We can wait for the rain to let up and, maybe, look for a better path where an actual route has already been carved through the thick brush."

"We're being followed?" Alexander asked. "Is that it?"

"Yeah. We are most definitely being followed. We're being watched."

"Natives?"

"Could be," he said. "Or jaguars."

Jaguars? Wonderful. Alexander did a slow three-sixty. The only thing moving were the thick leaves under the weight of water. "I don't see anything. I thought jaguars were solitary? They don't hunt in packs."

"They don't. Unless it's mating season."

"When is mating season?" Alexander asked.

"Whenever they are in the mood," the guide grinned. Alexander did not laugh.

The guide continued, "Look, this is your expedition. You paid me to lead you through the forest and for me to advise you and your team."

"And your advice?" Alexander said.

The guide held up a finger. He took a long moment and surveyed the area, spinning in a slow and deliberate circle. "Yeah. I'm pretty confident that we've been surrounded. If we keep on moving deeper into the forest, they are not going to give up and go away. This is their home, their terrain. We are the intruders. They are going to continue to track us, and when the time is right, like when we are all asleep, that is when they will attack."

"That's if it's a jaguar?"

"That's if it is anything. Once the sun goes down, we're going to be forced to make camp wherever we are at that time. We'll be in the open, vulnerable." The guide lowered his weapon some. He stood ready, though. His finger resting on the trigger guard.

Alexander exhaled. He removed his plastic-wrapped map. The guide was right. They were countless miles away from where the temple should be, and only a few miles from where they'd left the river boat anchored along the riverbank.

Alexander wanted to press on. As far as they were from the temple, they were the closest he'd ever been to the treasure. The thing was, being surrounded was not good. "Yeah, but you don't know by what?"

The guide cocked his head to one side, as if suddenly confident. "It's—"

Something cut a path through the forest, toward them. It was not being quiet about it, either. Branches snapped, leaves rustled, and low growls and snarls came from all around them. It could not have been a single jaguar, or even two. Whatever charged in their direction, it came at them fast. Determined.

"Retreat!" the guide shouted.

Retreat? Alexander thought. What in the hell could they do? There was but one path cut through the trees leading back to the river. "Everyone, back to the boat!"

They did an about-face, and ran. The going was tough, the footing muddy. The ground sucked at Alexander's shoes. It was as if they attempted a sprint through molasses while batting giant leaves and springing branches out of the way. It was no surprise when someone tripped, fell. Alexander grabbed Jeremy by the shoulders and tried pulling him back up to his feet. "Get up! Get up!"

The guide ran past them.

Once Jeremy was standing, Alexander pushed him forward. "Go, go."

Alexander had no idea what they were running from. He hadn't seen a single animal, or person, for that matter. He'd, unmistakably, heard the growling and snarling, though.

All he knew for sure was if his guide was turning-tail in an attempt at escaping, then so was he. There would be time for questions later. Hopefully.

Once again, only the sound of his heart slamming in his chest and his breathing filled his ears. Tunnel vision obscured his view. He saw only what was in front of him. Ducking from swinging branches, jumping over fallen trees, and trying not to get tripped up by the snaking vines became the objective. The obstacle course held potentially deadly consequences.

Alexander stumbled. He realized he was the last in the pack. If he went down, there was no one behind him to pick him up. He had lost sight of both Nicholas and Jeremy. He prayed they'd make it safely to the river, regardless.

As if he'd jinxed himself, Alexander toppled over a raised root. It grew from the mud like a noose for his foot. He went down fast and hard, burying his face in mushy mud. He struggled getting up onto his elbows, and struggled more as he wiped muck from his eyes.

Once on his feet again, Alexander could only see the blur of a path ahead. He blinked hard, and shook his head. The mud was in his eyes.

He launched himself forward. One foot after the other, he ran as fast as the insufferable terrain allowed.

He realized he'd lost his machete. Probably dropped it when he fell. He only recognized the loss because he uselessly fought cutting his own path through the jungle. Alexander did the next best thing: he shielded himself with an arm, tucked in his head, and pushed through the dense, dark green growth. The distance he traveled without the long, sharp blade hadn't been easy. He wasn't sure how he'd strayed off the initial path in the first place.

While the rain kept most of the insects and creatures at bay, whatever still chased him through the trees wasn't put off by the downpour.

He wished he knew what he was running from. Would it make any difference? He supposed not. If something chased him, he ran. Simple.

It was then that he heard something growl. He couldn't escape the horrid thoughts filling his mind. He envisioned claws latching onto his back, raking through flesh and ripping him open. He imagined the weight of a beast driving him into the mud, face-first, and tearing him apart while trying to sink giant fangs into the back of his neck.

Somewhere in front of him was the rest of his team. Had they scattered? Would any of them make it safely back to the boat?

A snapshot of Pricilla filled Alexander's thoughts. A solid image of her smiling face. When she looked up at him, he saw the love in her eyes, and the way she smiled. It was as if she couldn't *not* smile at him. He only hoped she saw the same in him when he was looking at her.

He was not going to die on this continent. He would make it back to the boat. He would make it back home.

Something jumped into the path in front of him. A large black blur. Where did it come from? Up in the trees?

The sight of the jaguar stopped him dead in his tracks: the black spots on almost shiny, yellow fur, shining green eyes, and large canine teeth in its jawline. He stood up straight.

This was it. The end.

And then he heard the gunshot. The sound of the rifle firing didn't echo in the jungle the way he thought it might. The humidity, the rain, captured the sound and made it reverberate flat.

The beast leapt out of Alexander's path and back into the brush. He had no idea if it was gone. He had no idea how many other jaguars were in pursuit. He did not feel as if he had survived anything, yet, other than one potential stroke with death.

He saw Jeremy ten yards ahead of him. "Come on, Alexander! This way!"

One of his friends had come back for him, God love him! "I'm right behind you!"

Jeremy turned, darting forward, and disappeared. Alexander waited one precious heartbeat to regain his bearings, then followed. He picked up speed. Ducking and jumping as best he could. He saw the back of their guide. He was catching up.

Running as fast as he could, Alexander did his best to ignore the urge to look behind him. He had to trust he wasn't being followed because, in truth, if something was about to get him, it *would* get him. He couldn't outrun a predator in normal circumstances. Serpentining through an overgrown forest was slow going at best. Trying not to trip over a root, or vines, was near impossible. Oh yeah, he thought, if something was about to get him, it *would* get him!

The muscles in his legs burned. He felt pain in his gut. He was pushing his body. There were limits. He was reaching his. Just when he was sure he could not continue, he saw it. A break in the trees. The clearing was ahead of them. Ahead of him.

Soon, he could see the boat. Their boat.

At the edge of the clearing, the first guide stopped, turned, and waved everyone on in encouragement. They had made it.

They had almost made it.

From the top of a tree, leaping off a branch, was another jaguar. Its body extended as it flew through the air, front claws extended. Jeremy had enough time to face his attacker.

The beast crashed into the man, knocking him to the wet ground. Alexander saw the silky leopard pattern, bright green eyes. Sleek muscles moved and tensed under tight skin as the animal's ears laid back against its head. It let out a high-pitched snarl before the jaguar buried sharp teeth into the man's throat.

One of the guides screamed, raised his rifle, and waved it like a flag. "To the boat! To the boat!"

Killing the jaguar was too little, too late. Jeremy was dead.

They raced around the bloody carnage and onto the boat.

On land, beyond the clearing, Alexander saw something. He squinted to peer through the downfall.

The boat engine started. The guide spun the galver. As they moved away from the bank, Alexander saw people.

A row of people with dark skin, faces painted, and holding spears. The spears were aimed at Alexander. Their arms were pulled back, as if they were about to throw the spears like javelins, and Alexander and the others were their target!

2

Rochester, NY - June 3 - Present day

"You are going to need money, Mr. Albright. There is no other polite way of putting this. I am not one to beat around the bush. I hope you can appreciate what I am telling you?"

Michael Albright pulled the cell phone away from his ear and looked at the screen, wrinkling his facial expression. "Yes. This, I know."

He shook his head, rolled his eyes but, in truth, he didn't know.

How much money would he need? It was too late for clarification. He'd already made himself sound cocksure. Just over twenty-one years old, and the last thing he wanted was to sound like a dumb kid when discussing plans with this guy. Michael was contracting the man as an employee. If Gregory Hanson didn't have confidence in his employer, the trip could wind up bust.

"I am talking about some serious cash. And it has to be cash. We'll be crossing borders. There will be road and water patrols. Guerrillas. That kind of thing. Easiest way through these, let's call them barriers, is with cash. Are we on the same page, Mr. Albright?" Hanson reiterated.

Michael leaned his weight against the high-back leather chair behind his father's desk. For a moment he thought about throwing his legs up and crossing his heels on the corner of the desk, but refrained. His father was not a tidy man, in fact he was more of a hoarder than anything, but Michael knew his father would never have tolerated feet on the furniture. Especially not in his study, and definitely not on his desk. This desk.

The laptop displayed Hanson's personal tour guide website. Beside the computer was Michael's father's ledger. It was opened to a page where the name Gregory Hanson had been written, with a question mark beside it, then the word "Guide" was underlined with four descending bold black lines.

He wondered if Hanson knew he didn't know how much money would be needed for the excursion.

"I have the money, Mr. Hanson. I understand what's involved. I am fully prepared." Michael figured he would make some calls, do some research. He'd seen movies. Money always smoothed the way through an otherwise secure, or bordered, location. He didn't think he would need to travel with tens of thousands of dollars in cash, but several thousand should do it. Large bills. Easier to carry, and conceal.

The ledger, a two-tone hardbound book, was a bit smaller than a spiral notebook. An old rubber band had held the book closed. It kept together the odd things his father stuffed between pages. There were pressed flowers, flattened insects, folded pages torn from other books and handwritten journals.

Michael opened the desk's center drawer, fumbled around with fingertips for a new rubber band, and tossed the bright green rubber band onto the desktop as a replacement. He stretched the old band between fingers. There was no snap left in its elasticity. Instead, the band broke.

Only quiet sounded from the other end of the line. "Mr. Hanson?"

"So, you're Alexander's kid. Is that right?"

"That's right. I am."

"Will the old man be joining us?" Hanson said.

"He passed away," Michael said. "Last month."

"Ah. I see. I'm sorry for your loss." Hanson cleared his throat. "Okay, Mr. Albright. You've got the money aspect covered. I'm trusting that you do. As long as you get what I'm telling you?"

"I do." He lifted the ledger and carefully flipped through the pages. Every page was filled with his father's handwriting. There were both legible and illegible scrawlings on the lines, in the margins, and even around most of the corners. Some pages contained pencil sketch drawings. The items depicted did not look familiar. Some things were circled countless times, underscored, or bolded from retracing the context over and over.

Blue ink. Black ink. Red ink. Lead pencil. Michael would

not be surprised if, when he had time to comb through every page of the ledger, he found some entries made in crayon. The thing was, this particular ledger was one of close to one-hundred similar logs.

The filled bookcases in the study contained archaeological, geographical, and geological textbooks. There were also stacks of National Geographic magazines (many containing articles written by his father over the decades), and on one shelf —eye level— stood his father's row of ledgers.

"Good. Then we will see you soon."

"We will be landing on the sixteenth," Michael said. He clicked onto the calendar tab. June sixteenth was highlighted. The plan was falling into place. He stood up, and walked around the desk. The gold-framed painting hanging on the wall had been mounted with hinges. Behind the painting, Michael's father kept a hidden wall safe. That was where he'd found this specific ledger, along with other peculiar items.

"My team and I will pick you and your guests up at the airport. Keep me posted on any flight changes. Otherwise, I look forward to meeting you," Hanson said.

"Okay, sir. See you in a few weeks."

"Ah, and the route you were interested in taking, Mr. Albright—"

"Yeah. Soon as we hang up I will snap off a picture and email it to you. I have your email here on the website."

"That should work, Mr. Albright. Once I have that I can get a better idea of what you're looking for, and I will send you a more specific quote, which will include the number of people on my team, the equipment —SUVs, a boat— that kind of thing."

Michael knew the cost of the trip rounded up to a small fortune. It should be worth the investment. He suspected Hanson wanted to remind him to pack a lot of cash. "Okay. Sounds good. I look forward to the estimate."

Michael ended the call as he closed the safe and pushed the painting back into place. After closing his laptop, Michael unzipped his backpack. He stuffed the laptop and his father's ledger into the pocket and then zipped it closed again. He slung one strap over his shoulder and left the study.

Next, he sent a group text to his girlfriend and three best

friends. *Everyone still good for tonight, right?* Send. As affirmative responses *ding*-ed in, he smiled and snatched his car keys from off the counter.

Activating the house alarm, Michael stepped outside, locked the front door behind him, and made his way to his car. As he backed out of the driveway, he stopped. This was the house he had grown up in. It still hadn't completely sunk in: Now it was his house. Five bedrooms. Two bathrooms. Two and a half car garage.

All of it was his.

3

It was nearly five. The sun shone brightly in a near-cloudless sky. For the end of May, it was already hot out. The temperature was in the mid eighties. Although a slight breeze flowed between tree branches, the increasing humidity stole any relief. It should have been a welcome change. Most of the month consisted of dark skies and rain. Lots of rain.

Michael Albright wanted some things for the evening. He'd already ordered pizzas. They would be delivered around eight. He stopped at the grocery store and picked up beer, tortilla chips, and salsa. In the check-out, he removed an energy drink from the glass encased fridge and added the drink onto the black conveyer.

Sticking the purchased items into the trunk, minus the energy drink, he sat behind the wheel, cracked open his drink, and took a long swallow. Starting the car, he decided on one more stop before heading home.

Driving along Elmwood Avenue, and just before the University of Rochester, Michael made a left hand turn onto Mt. Hope, where the Victorian cemetery of the same name contained the remains of his father. It was hard to believe over a month had gone by since his father died.

In the center of Mt. Hope Cemetery one could find plots hundreds of years old. The engravings on slabs of weathered tombstones were barely visible. Hills and valleys made exploring the cemetery an enjoyable experience for dog walkers and historians. Tall archaic-looking trees and monster movie-like mausoleums made for the perfect location for midnight parties and rituals.

As the plots unwound from a tight spiral, the dates on the markers decreased. While Michael was set on cremation when he died, his father had already bought a modest mausoleum. Michael knew the archaeologist in his father was *where* the decision came from. His father had not been an Egyptologist or into hieroglyphics but, on some level, it was always about burials, bones, and preservation.

Maps from the front office could be obtained. Every marker was well plotted and easy to find, once you understood the legend in the bottom right corner. For visiting his parents' mausoleum, Michael did not need a map. He drove his car and parked at the corner of Grove and Beech.

The mausoleum bore the Albright name over the locked entrance. At the top of two steps was a slate "porch", with a pillar on either side of the doorway. The structure resembled a popular Tiny House seen on the Discovery Channel. An entire house condensed into five hundred square feet or less.

"Hey, guys," Michael said, as he set down his backpack and sat down under the leaves of a Northern Red Oak. He rested his back against the base, his elbows up on his knees. He held the energy drink in both hands between his legs.

The shade under the tree brought relief from the sun, but escaping the humidity was still not possible.

"I know, I know. You're wondering why I'm here, *again*, aren't you?" He laughed, and then took a sip from his drink.

Although his mother passed away when Michael was four, and he didn't really remember her on his own, his father always told him stories about her, and of them. He loved hearing about his mother —how the two of them met, when they fell in love, how they got married and, best of all, stories about when he had been born.

"I can't stay long. Everyone's coming over tonight. I have to get back home and clean up a little. I just, sometimes, I can't drive by here and not stop in to say a quick hello.

"But, Dad, there's something else. I found your ledger. The one you kept in the safe. You were onto something, weren't you?"

Michael pursed his lips. "Of everything we talked about, how come you never mentioned this before? Any of it. Why would you keep this part of your life from me? I mean, I don't think you did it on purpose . . . or did you?

"It doesn't matter. I mean, it does. It matters." He lowered his head. His hair fell into his eyes. He brushed back his hair with a hand and looked straight at the Albright name on the mausoleum. "I'm going there, Dad. I'm going there and I am going to finish what you started. I am going to see this thing through."

Michael unzipped his backpack and took out his laptop. He used his cell phone's hotspot to gain access to the internet. He took out his father's ledger and set it on the grass beside him while the computer booted up. "If it's okay, I figured I could just do some research out here and hang out for a while with you guys. A little hot, but too nice a day to sit inside the house by myself."

He smiled, taking comfort in the moment because, for the moment, he didn't feel so alone.

4

Michael set plates and napkins around the table in the dining room. The center piece was a bowl of tortilla chips, with a personal bowl of salsa in front of all five chairs. The pizza arrived before his friends, but that was okay. He stuck the box in the oven to contain as much heat as possible.

Pacing by the foyer front door, Michael ignored the original Henri Clay Work grandfather clock in the corner, and instead checked his cell phone for the time again, and again. He thought, if anything, his girlfriend, Amber Wu, would have been early. She worked long hours riding on an ambulance as an EMT, emergency medical technician, and was taking extra classes to earn her paramedic degree. Her goal after graduation was med school. She had been dreaming of a career as an emergency room resident since junior high.

Michael stopped at the mirror by the coat rack. He hunkered down and moved closer to his reflection. He finger-brushed the top of his dark brown hair. He kept it short, nearly shaved on the sides. It was longer on top. Long enough to flop down over his eyes if he didn't gel it up into place. His thick eyebrows matched his hair, and sat perfectly over crisp blue eyes. He looked exactly like his father, when his father had been twenty-one.

Michael heard the souped-up engine of the sports car well before the doorbell rang.

Michael shot up straight, spun around toward the door, and adjusted his collar with both hands. He knew why his anxiety spiked, but reminded himself to breathe. These were his best friends. He could sell them on the idea. He knew it wouldn't take much convincing on his part. This is how they were. A Three Musketeers kind of bond. One for all, and all for one.

He opened the door, expecting Amber.

Instead, before him stood Tymere Evans and Natalie Payne.

Unlike Amber, who Michael had gone to high school with, he met Tymere and Natalie freshman year. They all lived on the same floor in the same dormitory on campus.

Tymere, with light brown skin, and caramel-colored eyes, reminded Michael of a model. His friend worked out every day, sometimes twice in one day. He wasn't bulky, but he was cut. Big biceps, six pack abs. It wasn't that Michael stared at his friend. Tymere insisted on wearing shirts half a size too small. When Tymere finished his business degree next year, he planned on attending law school. The goal was to become a sports agent. He saw the movie Jerry Maguire and heard the steady *ca-ching* of money-making opportunities. The career path definitely matched the personality. Michael knew somehow, someway, Tymere would find a way to shout "show me the money" at a ball club on behalf of one of his clients. And then their rat pack would have to hear all about it everytime they got together.

"Mikey! What's going on?" Tymere said, as the two hugged hello. They always hugged hello.

Michael stood aside, letting them into the house. "I have just been pacing back and forth, waiting for everyone to get here."

Tymere turned and faced Natalie. "We know you aren't lying. You need, like, some O.C.D. meds or something. Look at you? You're all wound up. It's killing me. I have to know what's going on. What is this all about?"

"Soon," Michael said, pulling Natalie in for a hug. He kissed her cheek. "Glad you guys made it."

Natalie was Tymere's polar opposite. The two had been dating since the end of freshman year. It surprised everyone. Her milky skin looked almost pasty under flaming orange hair. Behind simple, thick, black glasses frames, Irish green eyes hesitantly watched the world. They took in everything. She rarely spoke. She always observed. Her opinions, her views, came out in bold paintings and sketches. Her artwork was her voice.

Tymere spun around the foyer. "What? Are we first? Where's Amber?"

"I haven't been able to reach her. She was working until about an hour ago. That's when her shift ended. You know how that goes. Last minute call. Tough with her schedule." Michael waved toward the other room. "I have some drinks out. Chips. Salsa. That kind of thing. Nat, I have some of those seltzers you like."

"Thank you, Mike."

"Sounds good," Tymere said. Natalie followed him into the dining area.

Tymere called out, "You make us dinner, Mikey?"

"Pizza." Michael checked his phone. "Marshall sent me a text about a half hour ago. He should be here any minute."

"Good deal. Good deal," Tymere said. "So what do you say? Give us a little hint about what's going on? I mean, you're being so secretive. That's not like you."

Natalie smiled. "We can wait until everyone gets here, Mike."

Tymere exhaled. His shoulders sagged. "Fine. Fine. We can wait. I'm not going to lie though. You have definitely piqued my curiosity."

The doorbell chimed.

Michael held up a finger. "All in good time."

He opened the door. Marshall Williams wore a white dress shirt, jeans, and suspenders. Although a bit overweight, his eccentric style absorbed some of the attention. He kept his coarse beard and mustache a bit long. It took him forever to grow the thing. There were still some thin, or bald-*ish* spots. He kept it long, and a bit unkempt, hoping the curly hair gave the impression of uniform hair growth. It didn't. "Mikey," he said, grinning. "Hope I'm not too late?"

They shook hands. "Right on time. Tymere and Natalie just got here, too."

Tymere and Natalie held up their drinks. "Marshall," they both said.

"Hey, guys." Marshall shook Tymere's hand, and hugged and kissed Natalie hello. "Drinks?"

They stepped aside and Marshall went into the dining area. "Whoa. Mikey, you cook dinner for us?"

"Pizza," Tymere answered.

Michael's phone chimed. He checked the display, but his smile faded. "Okay, Amber is running late. She said to start without her. We can do that. Eat, anyway. No sense letting the pizza go cold."

"It's here already? The pizza?" Marshall asked.

"Have a seat. It is in the kitchen. I'll grab it."

"You going to tell us what's going on, why the secret meeting?" Marshall said. He cracked open a beer and sipped at the foam on top of the can, then licked the foam off his upper lip.

"Let's eat," Michael said. "I really want to wait until Amber is here."

"Does she already know what this is all about?" Tymere asked.

"She doesn't."

Natalie puckered her lips, but didn't say anything.

"Damn," Tymere said. "Now I am really dying to hear what's what."

The four of them sat around the dining room table, eating pizza. Michael was too nervous to eat. He put some chips on his plate. He ate them without salsa. After draining his first beer, he went into the kitchen and picked up a fresh drink for everyone.

While in the kitchen, he heard the front door open and then everyone greeting Amber. He opened the refrigerator and snatched up an extra beer for his girlfriend. Hands full, he pushed through the swinging door and re-entered the dining room.

Amber, still in her ambulance uniform, smiled. "I am so sorry I am late."

Her long, straight raven black hair was tied off in a ponytail. She had unbuttoned her blue dress shirt with a gold nameplate over the breast pocket and corp patch on the shoulder. She shrugged off the shirt, and tossed it over the back of her chair. Underneath she wore a black EMT t-shirt. Her wardrobe consisted of mostly EMT, fire department, and police t-shirts. "Caught a call ten minutes before the end of shift. Suicidal male. Police didn't get on scene until twenty minutes later. They had us stage down the street for nearly an hour, then sent us back in service. I figured, the way you've been acting lately, I'd skip going home and showering and just come right here."

He moved in for a kiss.

"Oh, no. I'm gross, but I will take one of these." She took a beer from him, popped it open, and drained most of the can in a gulp. "I'm starving."

Michael set down the other drinks for everyone, and clapped. "Let's eat."

Tymere pushed back in his chair. "We can eat. Amber, honey, eat. But Michael, c'mon, son. What the hell is going on?"

5

Michael stood at the head of the dining room table. His friends sat around, staring at him, waiting. He made eye contact with each of them, then turned and looked at his laptop and his father's ledger on the small hutch behind him. "Okay, I know you are all wondering why I called everyone together tonight."

Tymere tossed his napkin onto the table. "Really?" He laughed. "You have a whole speech prepared, don't you?"

Natalie slapped Tymere's leg. "Give him a chance. I like the theatrics. It builds suspense." She wrung her hands together. "Anticipation is so intense."

Michael raised his eyebrows. "Can I continue? Hmm?"

Tymere laughed. "Stage is all yours."

"Thank you," he said. "Okay. Like I was saying, I know you are all wondering why I planned this tonight. In just a few months, we will be entering our senior year of college."

Marshall let out a whoop whoop. Tymere joined in.

Natalie and Amber laughed.

Michael raised his beer. "A well deserved toast to our senior year."

They all raised their drinks. "To senior year," Tymere called out.

"Hear, hear." Amber nodded approvingly, and finished her beer. "I need another one."

"Wait, wait," Michael said. He desperately wanted to continue. "Okay. Hold on."

He went through the swinging door and returned with another round of drinks for everyone. "We good? Everyone has enough to drink?"

"I'm sorry, honey," Amber said. "Something tells me I am going to need a little buzz for whatever surprise you have coming our way."

"Hear, hear," Natalie joined in. Everyone laughed.

Everyone, except Michael.

"Guys," he said, trying to get back on track.

"Sorry," Amber apologized.

"It's okay," Michael said.

Amber looked around the table. "But I'm right, right guys?"

"Hear, hear," the others chanted.

"You know what," Michael said, and turned away.

Amber stood up and went to him. "I'm just kidding. I'm joking. Please, continue. I can honestly say you have our attention. You do."

"Alright." Michael hugged Amber. "Please. Sit down. Sit. Please."

When she sat down, Michael decided on a slightly different tactic. He reached for the ledger. He held it closed in a hand the way a preacher might hold a Bible while addressing his congregation. "Next year will not be easy. We will be tied up taking classes. Applying to med schools," he nodded toward Amber, "and law school," he nodded toward Tymere. "Natalie is always talking about moving to New York City and starting up an art gallery."

"I'm not unrealistic," Natalie said. "I fully expect my IT degree to pay the bills."

"You're an amazing artist, honey," Tymere said.

"You are, you truly are talented," Michael said. "And Marshall will be going for his masters in teaching, and I . . . I'm going to declare a major."

"I know you will, honey," Amber said. She jabbed fingers playfully into his side. "Eventually."

Michael waved his hands in surrender. "Ouch. Low blow, dear. Low blow," Michael said. "The point is, this is it. Right now. This is it."

"What does that even mean?" Tymere asked.

"It means, this time next year, nothing will ever be the same. The five of us will be headed off in different directions. I am confident we will always be best friends, but time and distance has a negative way of impacting things," Michael said.

"Honey, don't say that," Amber said.

"Yeah, man. That's kind of a buzz kill," Marshall agreed.

"That's why this summer, right now, we have to do something completely crazy," Michael said. "We need—no—

we *deserve* to do something epic!"

"What, like matching tattoos or something?" Tymere asked. "I'm not getting a tattoo."

"No. Not like matching tattoos," Michael said.

"Good," Tymere said. "Because I'm not getting one."

"I'm not talking about tattoos. I'm talking about an adventure."

"Like a trip?" Amber asked.

Michael pointed at Amber. "Exactly. Like a trip."

"A vacation?" Natalie asked. "I don't know that I can afford anything bougie right now."

"Not a vacation," Michael explained. "An adventure."

"What did you have in mind?" Tymere asked. "I know you have something planned. And that journal tells me you have been thinking about this for awhile. How old is that thing?"

"I didn't know you journal*ed*," Amber said.

"I don't. It's not mine. It's my father's," Michael said. "I propose an all expenses paid trip to Brazil, into the heart of the Amazon."

Tymere shook his head. "Brazil?"

"What do you mean, 'all expenses paid'?" Natalie asked.

"Wait, like, *the* Amazon - Amazon? Like the rainforest?" Tymere asked.

Michael sat down at the head of the table. He set his father's ledger down in front of him. "Let me tell you a story, all right?"

"A story?" Amber said.

"Hear me out, see, there was this pirate—"

"Wait." Tymere held up his hands. "A pirate?"

Natalie clapped a hand over Tymere's arm and lowered his arm back down. "Are you going to let him talk, or what?"

"Sorry. Sorry," Tymere said.

"Thank you, Natalie." Michael cleared his throat. "Like I was saying. There was this pirate. Roche Braziliano. That wasn't his real name."

"That's a relief," Tymere said, then held up his hands again. "Sorry. Sorry."

Michael ignored his friend. "It was most likely Gerrit Gerritszoon."

"Gerrit ... Gerritszoon? Mikey, are you making all of this up?"

"Are you going to let him talk?" Natalie looked upset. She folded her hands into her lap, and leaned forward. "If he has one more outburst I'm clocking him in the head with a beer can."

Tymere used an imaginary key and locked his closed lips.

"There is not a lot written about this person. He was a pirate from 1654 until around 1671, when he disappeared at sea. The thing is, he started out as a privateer in Brazil, and didn't go full-blown pirate until he eventually moved to Jamaica. That was in 1654."

"Wait," Marshall said. "What's the difference between a pirate and a privateer?"

"That's a good question," Michael said. "A privateer is someone who pretty much behaves like a pirate, but under the commission of war. So it is almost like they have governmental authority to attack other ships and steal and kill because there is a war taking place. They weren't an official Navy. They were private ships and sailors hired to patrol the sea on behalf of the nation. Then the government would reap the rewards of the attacks. Except, the privateers ended up keeping and hiding a lot of the gold and jewels for themselves before turning anything over to the government."

Michael took a sip of beer, wiped his forearm across his mouth, and held back a burp. "Excuse me. Okay. From what I could find out, Roche was quite notorious. He attacked enemy ships and allied ships, killing everyone on board, and then stole whatever valuables he found. He collected fortunes in treasure for the Brazilian government. Eventually, he realized there was no reason to give away everything he worked so hard, and risked his life, to steal—"

Natalie kept nodding her head. "Which is why in 1654 he decided to go full-blown pirate and move to Jamaica?"

"Exactly!" Michael was out of his chair, hands planted on the table.

Amber pointed at the ledger. "What's in the journal?"

"So, you all know my father was a professor," Michael said. "What you might not have known is, before I was born, he was an archaeologist. Like, he went on excursions to find remnants of lost and ancient civilizations. He uncovered pottery, chiseled weapons, and slabs of rock with symbols and forms of primitive writing on them. A lot of his discoveries are sitting in museums around the world. He has had hundreds of articles published in magazines like National Geographic and the Smithsonian."

"And the journal?" Amber asked a second time.

Michael sat back down. He opened up the ledger and carefully removed a folded piece of paper.

The others stood up. Their eyes focused on the paper centered on the table. They leaned over it, taking it all in.

"What is that?" Marshall asked. "Is that South America?"

Michael said, "It is."

"Is this a map? A treasure map?" Tymere said.

"That's right." Michael smiled. "See this here, and here? It's the path my father took. He traveled down the Amazon River to the Xingu River—"

"Xingu?" Tymere asked.

"It's spelled X-I-N-G-U but is pronounced Sheen-goo," Michael explained. "This is the path my father took, and then, this part of land here? That is Koatinemo. My father documented the journey there."

"What did he find?" Tymere asked.

"That's the thing. This ledger? It has all this information about a huge booty—"

Marshall laughed. "That sounds right, dude. Booty."

"It's what pirates called their stolen treasures," Michael explained.

"Yeah. No kidding. But when you say it, it just sounds stupid," Marshall said.

"I agree," Tymere seconded.

"Fine. Whatever," Michael said. "The point is, supposedly there is some temple covered by growth, or inside some cave— my father wasn't sure. And that is where the Pirate Roche hid his biggest boo—um, stolen treasure."

"But your father didn't find it?"

"Nothing to indicate he did. In fact, of all of his ledgers out on display in his study, I found this one hidden in a wall safe. Guys, I think he planned to go back and finish the expedition. But then he got too old. And now, well. Now he's gone." Michael sat back in his chair. "He left me the combination for the safe in his will. He wanted me to find this ledger, and the other things he had stuffed into that safe."

"You think your father wanted you to go out into some

jungle to hunt for buried treasure?" Amber asked. She sounded sincere. Michael still felt a slight sting of mocking.

"Yes."

"He was an archaeologist. He did this kind of thing all the time, right?" Tymere pursed his lips together for a moment, and then relaxed his expression. "Look at me, okay? I wear Italian dress shoes and Gucci suits. Does it look like I even own clothing made for traipsing through a rainforest? I'll answer that for you. It doesn't, because I don't own jungle clothing. For a trip like you're talking about, I would need an entirely new wardrobe."

"When did you want to go?" Natalie asked.

Michael grinned. "Next week."

6

"Can I show you guys something else?" Michael led them into the basement, switching on lights at the top and bottom of the staircase. The basement *could have* resembled a nightclub, the available space more than abundant. Michael easily envisioned an L shaped, fully stocked wet bar, sporting a mirrored barback. Plenty of room for card tables and chairs, not to mention a digital jukebox, electronic dart board, and a full-size billiards table. The remodeling possibilities were endless.

Instead of a party room, a row of low wattage naked lightbulbs, with pull-string switches, lined the basement ceiling. On either side of the row of dim lighting, Alexander Albright installed wire, four-shelf racks, and then proceeded to fill each shelf with an array of storage boxes. Each box, although meticulously labeled, meant absolutely little to Michael.

Leaning against the second rack on the right were five, stuffed-full, hiking backpacks. Additional gear, stored in two unzipped duffel bags, sat just in front of the backpacks. Above each backpack, on a corresponding Albright storage box, sat a stack of folded khaki utility pants, matching vests, colored t-shirts, and brand new hiking boots.

Tymere touched the tongue of a boot. "Mikey, what's all of this?"

Natalie knelt in front of a backpack, unzipped the top flap, and rummaged around inside. She removed a sheathed machete and held it up by the rubber handle. "You aren't kidding about this, are you?"

Amber, beside Michael, slipped an arm around his waist, while the other, bent at the elbow, allowed for nibbling on the corner of her thumbnail. "Sweetie, what exactly are you up to?"

Marshall, who sat on the floor, had removed his shoes and was trying on a pair of boots. "These fit perfectly!" He stood, then laced them up tight. "I mean perfectly."

"When I said all expenses paid, I meant it." Michael picked up the first backpack, slung it over his shoulders, and belted the harness across his waist. "I already bought all the supplies we would need for this trip. Including clothing, Tymere. In each bag you will also find the, 'er, unmentionables. Boxer briefs. Bras. That kind of thing."

"Are you serious?" Amber asked. Curiosity snatched up her attention. She pointed at a backpack. Michael pointed toward the one next to where his backpack had been. She opened the bag and rifled around inside. She pulled out a matching bra and panty. "Oh, these are sexy."

"This will not be about sexy," Michael explained. "It is about comfort and practicality."

"Dude," Tymere said. "You spent a lot of money. I can see that—"

"I already bought the plane tickets. Round trip."

Marshall whistled in astonishment.

Tymere groaned. "Are you kidding me? Are you messing around with us right now? That was pretty presumptuous. Are they refundable tickets?"

"I'm not messing around with you. I'm dead serious. And no, they are not refundable."

"Here's the one thing that sticks in my mind about this whole thing, okay? If there is some lost treasure, some pot of gold that some pirate buried over four hundred years ago, then why didn't your father find it?" Tymere asked.

"I don't know."

"If he documented his expedition in that journal you found, and he was that close to actually finding the treasure, why didn't he ever go back and get it?"

"I can't exactly answer that," Michael said.

"Have you read the whole thing?"

"I have. A lot of it doesn't make a lot of sense—"

"That's not very encouraging." Tymere picked up a pair of the khakis and let them unroll as he held them up against his body. "Size looks about right."

"Toward the end of the ledger, after it seems my father was back home, he writes about my mother. She was pregnant with me. He also mentions being offered a full-time teaching position at the University of Rochester," Michael said, by way of explanation.

"A new wife. A kid on the way. It makes sense," Marshall said.

"Does it make sense that an ancient explorer walks away from a potential monumental find? Mikey, your dad has found a lot of cool shit over the years, right? And every find generated how many different articles? I mean he wrote a ton of articles on his expeditions, didn't he?" Tymere asked.

'That's true. He would document the preparation for, during, and after the expedition. He would switch around some content and could then resell the article he'd written to a variety of publications," Michael said.

"Not to mention speaking engagements. He toured the college circuit, talking in front of thousands of students during most of the school year, didn't he?"

"I didn't realize you knew so much about my father," Michael said, appearing both impressed and suspicious.

"Yeah, well," Tymere said. "I have read some of his stuff over the years."

Natalie stared up at Tymere, eyes and jaw open a little wider than usual.

"Wait," Marshall said, and clapped his hands. "Are you a *closet* archaeology enthusiast?"

"I've caught him watching the Discovery channel on more than one occasion," Natalie volunteered.

"I'm not answering that," Tymere said, his eyes locked on Natalie's. He did not appear thrilled she had called him out in front of everyone. "At least, I'm not answering until you can tell me how someone like your dad would leave an undiscovered treasure unfound. Because, in my mind, I don't see that happening. I don't see him giving up, hanging up his Indiana Jones hat and whip, and settling down to teach one-oh-one classes."

"I can't answer it, Tymere. But I can tell you this," Michael said. "I can tell all of you this. What I said upstairs hasn't changed. This could very well be our last summer together. If I sat back and let things play out, we wouldn't go anywhere this summer. Would we? We would all get too wrapped up in our own things—"

"Which is how life goes," Marshall said, shrugging.

"True," Michael agreed. "But I wanted to interfere. I figured I would step in and shake things up. Come on, guys. This is it. Our last chance to do something completely reckless and wild together. Do you know how memorable this trip will be, how epic an adventure this could be? We are talking about a possible once in a lifetime experience. Something we can do together as best friends."

"It really could be epic," Marshall said. "Dangerous and crazy, but epic."

"What if we don't find the temple, or treasure?" Amber asked.

"Who cares?" Michael said. The group stared at him. The shocked expressions were obvious. "That's right. Who cares? Because really, Tymere is right. Why would my father just walk away from the potential for unlimited wealth and fame? He wouldn't. Not my dad. Something stopped him from going back and finding that treasure—"

"Or he found out there was no temple, no pirate's booty," Amber said. "Yeah, you guys are right. That word just doesn't feel … natural. Booty." She shivered.

"Not at all," Natalie said. "I think we need a pact. No one should ever say booty."

"Here's the thing. I am going," Michael said. "This ledger is not complete. For some reason it was the only ledger in my father's safe. He wanted me to find this. I think he wanted me to go to Brazil and search for answers. I'm sure of it."

"I don't know if I can get time off from work," Amber explained. "For the summer, I am riding with two different ambulance corps. You know how summers are. We're busy all the time. It is like every night is a weekend during the summer."

"We'll only be gone for two weeks," Michael said. "Two weeks."

"Brazil?" Natalie said. She seemed like Michael's best ally at the moment. She had not uttered a word of complaint. If anything, she proceeded consistently with an open mind. 'The Amazon."

Michael couldn't help but grin. "Brazil. The Amazon."

"We're looking for some temple buried underneath overgrown jungle?" she asked.

"That's what I'm thinking."

"Tickets are already bought and paid for?"

"That's right. They are bought and paid for." Michael felt Amber's arm tighten around his waist.

Natalie said, "I'm in."

Michael gave her a high-five. "Who else?"

Marshall shrugged. "Sounds better than anything else I might do this summer. I was supposed to start at Walmart on Monday."

"You were?" Tymere asked.

"Don't knock it. The pay's good."

"I wasn't. You just never mentioned it before," Tymere said.

"I really don't want to work there. I will tell them about this unexpected trip. It might cost me my job," Marshall said. "But you know what? What the heck. Count me in. Worse case? I will find something different when we get back. There are a ton of places hiring right now."

Natalie rubbed her hands together. "If we find a treasure chest, you might not need some mangy *part-time* job."

"That is true, you know. Very true. And I like the way that sounds. Remember that movie with Nicolas Cage, National Treasure? Riley got to keep one and a half percent of the treasure they found. Remember that? You know how much that one and a half percent equaled? Like fifty million dollars. *Fifty million.*" Marshall ran his thumbs along the inside of his suspenders, tugging the straps away from his body as he did so. "That's not too shabby, right? I could see fifty million as life changing."

Michael eyed Tymere. "Ty? You in, or are you out?"

"This is the jungle we're talking about, right?"

"It is."

"I mean, isn't everything in that place trying to kill you? Will everything in there be trying to kill us?" Tymere folded his arms across his chest.

"I don't know about that—"

"In the rivers there are anaconda, right? The thing about those snakes is, they don't have fangs. No fangs, but if they get the chance to wrap around you, they'll squeeze the life right out of you. Know how big an anaconda can get? A male can grow to thirteen feet and a female, twice that."

"I don't—that's now how guessing works," Marshall said.

"What?" Tymere asked.

"Well. You asked us if we knew how big an anaconda can get, but then you didn't even pause. You just told us the answer. That's not how guessing works."

Tymere, who had been nodding his head, now bit down on his upper lip as he turned his attention back on Michael. "And alligators?"

Michael said, "Black Caiman."

"Giant alligators, then. We're talking about a twenty foot prehistoric maneater. They don't just swim fast. They are fast on land, as well. And because they're nocturnal, if we were to camp anywhere by the water, we'd better learn to sleep with one eye open," Tymere said.

"Ty—"

"And Jaguars?"

"They live in the jungle, yes."

Tymere held out a hand, and counted off. "There's the wandering spider, deadly."

"Whoa. I am not big on spiders," Marshall said.

"No?" Tymere said. "Well, that's what they have in the rainforest: big spiders, and Dart frogs. Piranha. You heard me. Piranha." Only the second time he said the name he broke piranha into three distinct syllables. *Pir - An - Haaaa.*

"I've seen a lot of shows," Amber said, "that pretty much say piranha don't really attack people. Not like in the movies. They don't just swarm in and eat the meat off a person who falls into the river in mere seconds."

"So you'd go swimming in, let's say, a pool filled with piranha?" Tymere asked.

"I would not." Amber arched her eyebrows.

"I rest my case," Tymere declared. "And let us not forget the twenty-four hour ant."

"The what?" Marshall asked.

"The twenty-four hour ant. They also call it the tropical giant ant. When it bites its prey, and that prey can be a person, it is said that it feels as if you are burning alive. They are, like, almost two inches big, these things. A two inch ant," Tymere said.

"You're not just an amateur archaeologist, are you? You're also like an entomologist?" Amber said.

"What's that?" Marshall asked.

"Someone who studies bugs," Tymere said. "And no. I am not. I just know a few things about what lives in the rainforest."

"Discovery Channel. I tell ya," Natalie pointed out. "Not to worry. I'll protect you."

"With a bow and arrow?" Tymere said. "Against an ant?"

"Bow and arrow?" Amber asked.

Natalie blushed.

"She was, like, an archery legend in high school," Tymere explained. "She even did shows at the renaissance festival in Sterling."

"I did not know that," Michael said. "Do you have a bow?"

"A recurve and a compound," Natalie said. "I can bring the compound, if you'd like?"

"I would," Michael said. "Well, Tymere. What do you say?"

Tymere shifted weight from one leg to the other. Arms, once again, crossed. "If there is even a remote chance of finding some buried treasure, even if it isn't this Pirate Brazil—"

Michael said, "Roche Braziliano."

"Roche *Whatever*. Even if there is a remote chance, no matter how small, then I have to come along so I can snatch up a piece of that pie. You know how expensive law school is going to be? Your father worked for the University of Rochester, so your tuition was basically free. Law school, on top of my undergraduate loans?" Tymere sighed. "I really do not want to be in debt until I die. I truly do not!"

"So," Michael asked. "Are you in, or what?"

"I'm in," Tymere agreed.

Michael slowly turned and fit his arms around and faced his girlfriend. "Amber, I know how important your work is, how much you love riding on the ambulance, but I am going to be completely honest. The trip really won't be the same without you."

He knew she understood he was going, with or without her. She did not seem to take the statement out of context.

"I'll get the time off."

Michael smiled. "So you're going?"

"I'm going," she said. They kissed and hugged.

"Guys, I am so excited. You have no idea." Michael squatted down. "Unpack your bags. Take a look at all of the equipment I bought!"

Natalie held up a baby blue cylindrical object. "What in the world is this?"

"A water purifier. You use it almost like a straw. This will let us drink from almost any water source and strain out any lethal bacteria."

"Lethal bacteria," Marshall repeated. With arched eyebrows, he pressed his lips into two straight, thin lines.

Tymere took in a deep breath, and as he exhaled, he mumbled, "I hope I don't live to regret this."

7

Amber stepped out of the bathroom wrapped in two towels. One swaddled her hair on her head, the other, held in place with a croner tuck, was just above her breasts. Michael had been on the bed, flipping through his father's ledger, but was distracted while she sang, showering. Now, her bare legs stole his attention.

The move from his bedroom into his father's master bedroom hadn't been an easy decision. Amber pushed him in the direction to swap out rooms. The attached bathroom was one of the main and most compelling reasons. The Couturier King Canopy bed, with hardwood frame and brass accents, sweetened the deal, from her perspective.

It felt unnatural; not sleeping in his father's bed, but sleeping with Amber in his father's bed. It just didn't feel right. Not at first. Little by little, he found himself more comfortable with the change. He couldn't deny how much he'd grown to appreciate having a bathroom right there.

Amber climbed onto the bed, holding her towels in place. "We're really going to do this, huh?"

"We are," he said.

"Go to the Amazon? Treasure hunting?"

"The whole sha-bang."

"The what?"

He shook his head, waving a hand. "Something my father used to say. The whole sha-bang. It means we're doing it all."

"I figured as much." She smiled, scooting back against the small stack of pillows. She brought up her knees and the towel slid down her legs, exposing thigh.

"I know you don't like taking time off from work." She paid her own tuition. Working hard was why she could afford electronic textbooks for class. Her parents didn't have the money to cover the costs. They helped as much as they could,

Amber paid what she could, and a mountain of student loans made up the difference.

"Why do you think, if your dad was so close to finding this place, he gave up?"

It was both an honest, and a very good question. Michael wondered himself. He flipped open the ledger. "The best I can guess is my mom."

"Your mom?"

"Yeah," Michael said. He didn't want her to freak out. She deserved as much truth as he could share. "Can I tell you something?"

"You know you can."

"Okay, look at this." He pointed to his father's last entry in the mysterious ledger.

She took the ledger. She stared at the page for a moment. "I can't read his writing."

"I guess Ph.D and M.D. have the same handwriting classes. I grew up with it, so I guess that makes me something of an amateur cryptologist."

She laughed. He loved when she laughed.

"On this, his last big adventure, my father and his team ran into some problems in the jungle."

"Problems?" she asked.

"It sounds like they ran into some kind of wild animal. One of the guides on the trip was killed. The rest made it out safely," Michael added, quickly. "But my father, who had just gotten engaged to my mother before the trip, decided he was going to hang up his exploration hat and focus more specifically on academia."

"Someone died from an animal attack?"

"That's what he said. My father wasn't overly sentimental. He didn't spend a lot of words explaining the situation. At least not in this book, but it was pretty clear it was his love for my mother that made him change careers," Michael said.

"Why didn't you tell the others this earlier?"

Michael closed the ledger. "I didn't want to scare them."

"You mean you didn't want them to say no," she said. "You basically manipulated your best friends into agreeing to do something that even your dad found too dangerous to attempt a second time."

She wasn't wrong. "Amber, I really need to do this."

"What about the others? Don't you think they deserve to know everything before they commit?"

Michael knew she was right. "I will tell them first thing tomorrow morning."

Amber sighed. "You promise?"

"Cross my heart."

"Let me ask you this: if we find this lost pirate treasure—"

"You wanted to say 'booty', didn't you?" Michael teased.

"I *so* did not!" She giggled. "I said 'treasure'. I meant treasure. Can I ask my question, Mr. Booty-man?"

"My apologies. Ask away." Michael closed the ledger and set it aside, giving his girlfriend his full attention. He even folded his hands into his lap, to punctuate the point.

"Marshall. He was talking about National Treasure. The money those guys got when they found some treasure—"

"Gold and jewels hidden by the Knights Templar. A series of clues taking treasure hunters on a grand journey across continents—"

"Whatever. You know what I mean. I saw the movie. They turned over the gold, after stealing the final piece of the puzzle—"

"The Declaration of Independence."

"Michael. Please," she said. "The thing is, they got paid when they turned over all the gold, right?"

"They did."

"Do you plan to turn over whatever treasure we find? Are you planning to keep it, and split it five ways?" She cocked her head to one side. "I'm actually surprised Tymere didn't bring this up when everyone was over."

Michael pushed up onto his knees, then pulled her into his arms. Despite her towels falling off, he stared directly into her eyes. Her wet hair fell down over his arms. "Are you worried, young lady, that I am gonna block you from an equal cut of the pie?"

"That was not what I was worried about." She bit his lower lip.

"Ouch!" Grinning, Michael pulled free.

"I want to know if we are keeping whatever we find, or doing like your father did, and giving the treasure to some museum?" she asked.

"My father turned all of the treasures he found over to museums, and made a pretty good living doing so," Michael said.

"He also was practically on staff as a writer for how many magazines?"

"That's true."

"When he went full time as a college professor, didn't he also do a college circuit tour, speaking at some of the biggest and best colleges around the country?" Amber asked.

"Around the globe."

"Around the globe," she repeated. "Is that what we're going to have to do to make a pretty good living?"

"You mean, as opposed to keeping whatever we find?"

"That's exactly what I mean."

Michael didn't have an answer. "The way I see it, the five of us will be in this together. I don't think it should be me who makes that kind of decision. Not on my own, without everyone first getting a chance to voice their opinion. Does that seem fair?"

"It does. It seems very fair."

"What would you do with the treasure? When we find it." Michael couldn't explain why he felt so confident about the expedition, but he was certain they would be successful. Maybe it had something to do with the investment, and the risk? He couldn't say for sure, but he knew they would be successful.

"I think . . . keep it."

"How do you make money from that?"

"Well, I mean, I would sell some of it. Or I have heard of, like, renting it out. Instead of giving the treasure to a museum, we charge the museums allowing them to display what we found," she explained. "Have you ever heard of anything like that before?"

"Actually, I have. I know there are people who own priceless paintings that do just that," he said.

"Maybe that is something we can propose to the group." Again, she cocked her head some.

Michael kissed her. They touched their foreheads together. "We can absolutely propose that idea. First, though, we have to find actual treasure. Once we have that in hand, then we can work out all of these details."

"But, you're pretty sure we're going to find something?"

"I am. I really am!"

8

Rochester International Airport

Michael and Amber shared an Uber to the airport. They packed light. It wasn't as if they could hike through the Amazon with a suitcase, even if that suitcase had wheels and a pull handle.

The backpacks Michael bought came stuffed full with most everything needed on the trip. He put all of the machetes into a locked suitcase he would check at the airline counter. There was no way they could bring the blades in the backpacks as a carry-on. Michael and Amber unloaded their luggage onto a baggage cart.

"I hope everyone gets here on time," Michael said. He kept looking around, as if his friends would pull up behind them. He thanked the Uber driver, then he and Amber pushed the cart through the automated doors into the airport.

"They'll be here," Amber assured him. "You texted them each a hundred times this morning. What did they say?"

"They said they'd be here."

She gave him a half-smile. "So there you go. They'll be here."

After checking the bags, Michael and Amber made their way through security. He removed his belt. They both removed their shoes. Their carry-ons passed through an x-ray as the TSA wanded them and waved them through,

"I have a bad feeling," Michael said. "They're not coming."

"Will you settle down? They're going to be here. Not everyone is almost three hours early to everything."

"I don't like to be late," Michael said. "It makes me apprehensive."

"Late? Do you understand just how early we are? You can't expect everyone to be neurotic about time like you." She might have been teasing, but she spoke the truth. Michael knew he arrived everywhere far too early, and usually wasted time waiting. If Michael missed the trailers in a movie theater before the show, he didn't stay for the picture. He would ask for a refund, and try again another time. It drove Amber nuts.

Someone shouted, "Mikey!"

At the back of the TSA line, Michael saw Tymere, Natalie, and Marshall.

Amber touched his arm. "What did I tell you?"

"I knew they'd come."

Their friends made it through the security check and joined them on the other side.

"See, babe," Tymere said, looking at Natalie. "Just like I said."

"You were right," Natalie said.

"Right about what?" Michael asked.

"I told her you'd be here way before us, and just standing right here watching for us like you were waiting for water to boil."

"Why are you always so early, Mikey?" Marshall asked. "I could have slept another two hours."

Michael checked his phone. "We've got two layovers. It's going to be twenty-four hours before we're in Brazil. You can sleep all you want."

# # #

In their seats on the airplane, Amber and Marshall watched movies on their tablets, using headphones so as not to disturb the other passengers. Tymere used a neck pillow and was sound asleep moments after takeoff. Michael sat by the window. He held his father's ledger in his hands as he stared at the clouds which resembled slow-shifting, snowy mountain peaks.

For the first time since deciding to take this trip, since convincing his friends to join him, Michael wondered if he had been right. Should they be doing this?

It wasn't in the ledger he carried, but Michael knew a little more about why his father never returned to Brazil for the treasure than what he shared with everyone. He recalled a time when he was much, much younger.

Company was over. His mother was serving coffee, and set out a cake she'd baked for dessert. Michael was supposed to have been in bed. He hated going to bed when there were visitors. He always felt like he was missing out. It was as if he knew the best conversations took place after he left the dinner table.

He was right, of course.

The two couples sat in the dining area, talking loudly. They laughed.

He was at the bottom of the stairs, crouched down low and peering around the corner into the dining room. The only light on was the one over the table. The rest of the house was dark, including the staircase where he hid.

The memory was so vivid. Every small detail about that night, except for his mother. She was a blur of an image. It was as if time slowly erased her from his brain. He had plenty of pictures of his mother. She had been beautiful, and had died far too young. Tall and thin, with long dark hair, he thought he looked more like his mother than he did his father. Other people either didn't see it the same way, or they, too, forgot what his mother had looked like. Everyone always told him he was the spitting image of Alexander, when Alexander had been his age.

He could hear her laugh, though. She laughed all of the time. The sound of her laughter was more music than anything he'd ever heard on a radio station. Or was that his memory playing tricks with his mind? Was anyone's laugh really musical?

"Alex, that time when we went to the Amazon?" the man at the table asked. Michael could not recall who the guests were that night. A man and a woman. They both had been dressed as if coming from a wedding. The man wore a sharp, black suit, and a white shirt with a thin black tie. Michael remembered the shine on the man's shoes, bright like mirrors. The woman wore a long, form-fitting red gown. The string of pearls matched the pearl bracelet on her left wrist. "To Brazil? I—I … How come we never went back?"

The laughter around the table halted. The mood in the room changed. Michael, for however young he had been, remembered the sudden shift.

Alexander placed a hand over his mother's hand. "You

remember what happened in the jungle?"

"Of course," the man said.

"Is any treasure worth dying for?" Alexander asked.

"Could have been a huge payday for us."

"Didn't we have enough huge paydays?"

The man shifted around on his chair, leaning forward, elbows now resting on the table. "Maybe for you. You have the articles, the public speaking—what do they give you? Tens of thousands for every college campus you visit? Me, the rest of us, we don't get any of that. We don't make a penny unless we find more treasures."

"I'm sorry, Nick. I am. I told you when we got back to the States, I'm done. I retired from that life," Alexander said. "One of our people died—"

"A guide died," Nick said. "A guide. Not one of us."

Michael's father tensed, but let go of Pricilla's hand. "I don't think you understand—"

"No," Nick said. His tone of voice was hoarse, sharp. "I don't think you do. I don't think you understand. Me, the others, we are all about the hunt. We need the hunt. Alex, if you won't lead another expedition, why not give us the map?"

"I'm not going to do that."

"Sell it to us, Alexander. We'll pay you a royalty on top of a fair asking price. How does that sound?" Nick's knee bounced. He appeared agitated, anxious.

Alexander stood up. "I will not be selling the map, Nicholas. Again, I am sorry. I think this evening has come to an end. I'd like for you and Sandra to leave now."

"You're being unreasonable, Alex."

"Please. I am asking politely."

"Nick," Sandra said. "Let's go."

The couple stood up.

Michael scooted backward up the stairs. He kept hidden in the shadows as best he could. He didn't fully retreat to his room, because there was no way he wanted to miss a thing.

"I have no idea why you are being so stubborn." Nicholas was close to shouting. Sandra tried reining him in, tugging on his arm, pulling him toward the front door.

Michael made eye contact with his mother. Somehow, even in the dark, she had seen him. Then she looked up toward his bedroom door. Without a word, he knew she wanted him to go back to his room.

He didn't budge. She folded her arms.

"I'm sorry you feel that way, Nicholas. But that is the last time I will tell you I am sorry. The natives, the animals, they didn't want us in that jungle. They made that perfectly clear. Going back would be a death sentence," Alexander said, positioning himself in front of Michael's mother. It was a protective stance.

Alexander didn't realize his mother seemed more interested in the fact Michael was hiding on the stairs than with the argument by the front door.

"Now, if you please? I think you should go," Alexander concluded.

Sandra opened the door.

Nicholas looked like he might give it one more try, getting the map, but refrained. Instead, he sucked in a deep breath and let out a long sigh. He took Pricilla's hand in his. Michael noticed the gold ring with black onyx and three small diamonds on Nicholas' ring finger. "Pricilla, thank you for a lovely meal. And I am sorry for ruining the evening."

"You're very welcome," Pricilla said. "You have nothing to apologize for. I know how passionate all of you are about your work."

"You're too kind," Nicholas said. He held out his hand. "Alex?"

Alexander did not shake Nicholas' hand. "Nick. Sandra. Drive safely, now."

When the front door closed, Michael spun around and, on all fours, sprinted up the stairs.

The natives, the animals, they didn't want us in that jungle. They made that perfectly clear. Going back would be a death sentence . . .

Michael never shared that with Amber, or Tymere, or Natalie, or Marshall.He never shared what his father said, and he never told them about after his father's funeral, when Nicholas contacted him.

About the map.

"Hey? Mike?" Amber pulled him away from his memories. "What were you thinking about?"

44

Shrugging, Michael said, "I was just watching the clouds."

"You were staring at the back of the seat in front of you." She put a hand on his leg. "You okay?"

"I'm fine. My brain is just running at a mile a minute. Logistics. You know?" Michael put his hand over hers. "What are you watching? Is that National Treasure?"

"Seemed appropriate." She gave him a kooky grin, eyebrows scrunched up over her brow. She offered up one of her ear buds. Michael took it, and stuffed it into his ear. They sat as close as they could with an armrest between them, and watched the film on her tablet.

Michael didn't focus on the movie. He couldn't help thinking he'd made a terrible mistake. Worse, he was responsible because now the terrible mistake involved all of his best friends.

9

Fortaleza, Brazil

The plane landed at the international airport without incident. Michael and his friends exited the plane and made their way to the baggage claim area. With the other passengers, they stood around the metal loop and waited as patiently as possible for the luggage to begin appearing on the motorized belt. Inside the airport, the temperature was cool, almost cold. Michael knew outside of the structure the heat and humidity was ready to welcome them to the equator.

Once the group had their bags collected, they stepped out of the comfort of the air conditioned airport and into the thick humidity. The *desembarque* area consisted of several lanes where someone waited to pick up family or friends. White and yellow cabs were parked in the far right lane, in case there was no one waiting. A bowed awning covered all of the lanes, blocking out the sun but not putting a dent in the heat. The air was thick, stagnant. There was no breeze. Michael was not surprised when his body immediately reacted. Desperate to keep cool, his body began perspiring. The drips started under his armpits and dots spotted his forehead.

"Now what?" Amber whispered.

Michael wasn't exactly sure until he looked around and saw a man standing between two identical black SUVs holding a sign: MICHAEL ALBRIGHT.

"Ah," he pointed out. "Our chariots await."

Michael waved an arm. No one said a word. Natalie and Marshall exchanged looks. Marshall mimicked Michael's arm wave. Giggling, Natalie wheeled her bags behind as she started toward the SUVs, Marshall in tow.

Tymere's left cheek twitched as he kind of stood on tippy-toes.

"You're not arching an eyebrow, Ty." Michael shook his head, attempting to hide a grin.

"Sure, I am," Tymere said, standing up taller on his toes. The left side of his face was scrunched together.

"That looks painful." Amber laughed, and patted him on the chest as she followed after the others.

"But, I'm doing it, right?" Tymere called after her.

Without turning back, Amber said, "Nope."

"I feel like you guys are just messing with me." Tymere stood on flat feet, but his face looked as if it were overcome with Tourette's-like ticks. "I'm telling you. I am arching my eyebrows."

Michael raised both of his eyebrows. "Yeah. You got it! You got it!"

"I do? I'm doing it?" Tymere sounded like an excited child who'd just won an elementary school spelling bee. "Am I really doing it?"

Michael jogged after Amber. "No, Ty. You're not."

Flustered, Tymere picked up his duffle bag and wheeled his suitcase along. "Whatever. You know what? Whatever."

Michael stopped in front of the man holding the sign with his name on it. "I'm Michael Albright."

The man stared at him for a moment. No words were spoken. He looked about forty-five years old. Solid build. It made Michael feel a little awkward. He didn't know Portuguese, and worried about effectively communicating with the people of Brazil.

"Michael. Ah, yes." The man lowered the sign. He had a well-trimmed dark beard, with wisps of grey at the chin. Thick eyebrows shadowed already dark, deep-set eyes. "I am Gregory Hanson. We spoke on the phone."

Immediately relieved, Michael tried not to make a show of exhaling. His relief was evident on his face. Hopefully it resembled heat rash instead of blushing. When they shook hands, Hanson's grip was firm, without crushing Michael's fingers in the process. "Very good to meet you. And this, this is my team. Tymere Evans, Amber Wu, Marshall Williams and, last, but absolutely not least, Natalie Payne."

Hanson shook hands with each person. "Ah, what's that?"

Marshall cocked his head, confused.

"That?" Hanson pointed at Marshall's chest.

"This? It's a GoPro." The camera was in a harness that he

wore over his chest.

"Yeah. We don't do that."

"Do what?"

"You can't film me. You can't film us," Hanson said. "We understand each other?"

Marshall looked over at Michael.

"Nah," Hanson said. "Don't look at him. Look at me. I'm the one telling you. No filming me or my people. We good?"

Michael stepped in. "We're just trying to document the adventure, you know? He won't film you or your team—"

Hanson shook his head. "The answer is no. No filming. Anyone or anything." He turned his attention back to Marshall. "Do we understand each other?"

Deflated, Marshall nodded. "I guess. Yeah."

Hanson stood there. Marshall stood there.

"Well?" Hanson said. "Are you going to take it off? It's hot standing out here. The SUVs are nice and cool. I can assure you."

Michael wasn't sure what transpired. Caught off guard, he watched the scene unfold. Amber tugged on his arm. He knew they needed Hanson and his team. The trip was dependent on their help. "Yeah. We got it. We get it. Marshall, take that off."

"Really?" Marshall asked.

"Really," Michael said. As Marshall set down his backpack, he removed the tiny video camera. "Sorry about that."

Hanson waved a dismissive hand. "No worries," he said, then turned and waved a come-here motion at the other SUV. Doors on the SUVs opened. A man and a woman climbed out.

"This is Chuck Neeson and Angelina Hamilton. They are a part of my team, and will be joining us on the excursion into the rainforest."

Once again, everyone said hello, and shook hands. Immediately after, Angelina and Chuck began loading the bags and gear into the second SUV. Hanson opened the back door of the first SUV. "Shall we? The A/C is on. And if you aren't already sweating, if we stand out here much longer, you soon will be."

Marshall climbed in first, making his way into the third row. Tymere sat in the third row with Marshall. Amber and Natalie sat in the middle row. Michael climbed up front, in the passenger seat, while Hanson went around to the driver's side. He strapped on his seatbelt as he asked if everyone was comfortable.

"Yes? Good. We can talk while we drive, yes?" Hanson asked. "I do not get down to Fortaleza often. When I do, however, I always enjoy Futuro Beach. Do any of you surf?"

Hanson watched Michael shake his head, then checked the rearview mirror for the response from the others. "Oh, that is too bad. I tell you the waves are perfect for beginners and skilled surfers. Depending on the time of day, and the season, of course. This coast is lined with beautiful beaches, dunes, sandstone and red colored cliffs. Beautiful. Simply stunning."

"What about food?" Marshall said. When the others groaned, he became defensive. "We've been flying for what felt like days. I'm tired of single-serve cookies and small cans of soda. I drink those in a sip. Look at me. Am I a small guy? Why on earth would you give me child portions?"

Hanson laughed. "I can feel your pain, Mr. Marshall."

"Just Marshall."

Michael could go for a good meal. He knew they picked on Marshall. That was unfair. His friend wasn't wrong. What they called meals on flights these days were not meals at all. They were barely snacks. Could be the difference between first class and coach. He'd have to remember that. The extra money per ticket would definitely be worth extended leg room and actual food and beverages.

"Marshall. What do you say we stop at one of my most favorite places to eat in all of Fortaleza? Then we will drop you off at your hotel. First thing in the morning we will head out to a smaller airport where I've chartered a helicopter to *Terminal Hidroviário de Altamira*."

"Helicopter?" Michael heard Amber whisper.

"You say your favorite restaurant in all of Fortaleza?" Marshall questioned.

"All of Fortaleza," Hanson assured them.

Balcone hosted an interior brick decor with exposed wooden beam rafters. The large group filled three rectangular tables pushed together into the center of the restaurant, along with an extra chair from a fourth.

"Now," Hanson said, "*Balcone* is a family run restaurant,

known for its Italian dishes, and its pizza. When it opened in two-thousand-fifteen, it was all about the pizzeria."

Hanson ordered h'orderves for the table, the Traditional Bruschetta. *Homemade bread with artisan tomato sauce, buffalo mozzarella, tomato confit, and pesto.* Michael thought it sounded delicious.

The menu was pretty extensive. While Michael wanted to be daring and try the Octopus a Provencal, or any of their seafood specialties, he was worried about his stomach. They had been traveling for a full day. It might be safer for his belly and his bowels if he went with something more familiar.

He and Amber decided to get a pizza with an array of veggie toppings with mozzarella. Natalie went with the Pomodoro with shrimp, which was a fettuccine in tomato sauce with ambados shrimp. Tymere ordered the marinated thigh fillet. Marshall went with a shrimp risotto with cream cheese and parma farofa, and a side of French fries.

Hanson and his team ordered two pizzas for the three of them to share.

Over beers, they all made small talk, slowly breaking the ice. Michael liked watching his friends interact with what he considered an almost imposing guide team. The three of them looked more militia than tourist guide.

He knew they weren't tourist guides, and if his friends had any questions on the matter, he was certain by now they also understood. Hanson and his team were there to get them through the jungle, while protecting them from the jungle itself, wildlife, and any dangerous natives.

When the food arrived, there were several moments where all small talk ceased. Food was passed around. There were plenty of oohs and aahs, yums and man-oh-mans. Everyone wore a smile.

Slowly, the conversations picked back up. Small talk, mostly.

Michael noticed the dynamics. Hanson and his team sat at one end, together. Hanson at the head of the table, using the extra chair. Angelina and Chuck sat across from each other. Although everyone mingled, Michael noticed those two, in particular, shared a lot of looks and knowing glances. What they knew, Michael hadn't a clue.

But he understood the looks. They weren't any different than the ones he saw Tymere and Natalie share from time to time.

This made Michael wonder if the two were not *just* peers, but a couple?

Amber, finished with dinner, leaving half a slice on her plate, dabbed a napkin at the corners of her mouth, and then cleared her throat. "Ah, Mr. Hanson—"

"I'm like Marshall, please," Hanson said. "Call me either Gregory, or Hanson. No mister is necessary. Far too formal. And I assure you, once we are miles into the jungle, formalities won't mean a thing. It is quite, how do I put this? Raw. It is very raw where we are going. So, if you will. Gregory or Hanson. I will tell you, my team? We usually go by last names. Like in gym class in high school."

Or the military, Michael thought. He didn't dare say that out loud. If anything, he was thankful Hanson and his team carried themselves the way they did. They had an aura about them. It was an opaque light that shimmied with a hint of danger. Or dangerous. Michael wasn't yet certain which fit more appropriately.

"Hanson, then," Amber said. "You mentioned something about a helicopter in the morning?"

"Ah, yes," Hanson said. "Michael has put us all up for the night at the Hotel Gran Marquise, not far from here. And then, in the morning, we are going to drive out to a friend's private little air strip. He has a helicopter and will pilot us across Brazil to the Amazon."

"That was what I thought you said."

"Not a fan of helicopters, Amber?" Hanson asked.

Although Amber had not expressly asked the guide to call her by her first name, it seemed apparent to everyone that they were all on a first name basis from this point forward. Except, Michael saw the way Amber almost winced when Hanson used her name.

He wasn't sure what caused the fraction of a reaction, but he caught it. For some reason, Hanson must have made her feel uncomfortable. Michael hadn't recalled witnessing anything happen between them. It was going to be tight traveling quarters for everyone. The last thing the journey needed was tension. He did not want his girlfriend feeling uncomfortable on this excursion. That would not be acceptable. Not at all.

"I'm not, Hanson. Not at all. Heights are not my thing. It isn't as obvious in an airplane, I suppose? But the idea of going up into the air in a helicopter gets to me. I'm not embarrassed to admit I am not thrilled about all of us crammed into a tin shell with one big blade rotating above our heads." Amber spoke calmly. There was no hint of emotion in her words. She gave her feelings in a matter-of-fact tone of voice.

Michael thought he figured out what had bothered Amber. Hanson called her by her first name after making a point of using the gym class comparison. However, Hanson had done it with Marshall, and with him, as well.

Not to mention the scene about the GoPro at the airport. Michael figured everyone was a little on edge. He knew he felt the tension.

"You all get a good night's sleep. I think come morning you might feel differently about helicopter travel." Hanson smiled a cocksure smile. It may have been a little smug, but it was not at all condescending.

Amber pursed her lips together. Her eyes opened a little wider, and she nodded in agreement. Michael almost laughed. She wasn't buying his 'get a good night's sleep and you will love helicopter' spiel.

10

Two Weeks Ago - New York State Museum

Located in the state capital was the New York State Museum. Out front was an expansive staircase and fountain. The inverted white design of the five-story structure was realized as a Beaux-arts style, in the Neoclassical tradition. Henry Hornbostle's architectural design is known for its thirty-six Corinthian columns, considered the longest colonnade in the world. The circular ground plan, the rotunda, rose from the second to the fifth floor, and was covered by a dome. Contained inside were more than fifteen million artifacts and specimens spread out across 130,000 square feet of exhibition space.

The curator's office, far less glamorous than the first floor, with its open space, high ceilings, and priceless artifacts, was located on the fourth floor. The gold name plate mounted on the wall beside the door, read: NYS MUSEUM CURATOR, and under that: DR. NICHOLAS KATIC, Ph.D.

As curator, Katic managed collections of works. He delegated the day-to-day chores of the care and display of items. He sat as head of a team charged with the design and creation of new displays for visitors.His biggest headaches came from fundraising and public relations. He loathed dealing with stakeholders, preparing budgets, and managing his staff.

Katic preferred more hands-on experience with the museum. Acquisitions, education, and research. Giving presentations and visiting other museums was something he still enjoyed. However, getting lost in deciphering ancient relics, as well as writing papers for publication, was where he now found his passion. As the museum grew, his role had become far more administrative than he liked. He missed the days when he wore an archaeologist's hat and explored the uncharted, dug up, priceless finds, and then delivered his discoveries to an old man with a gold curator name plate outside an office door.

Time was not constant. The older one became, the faster it moved. That was not a myth, but a fact. Any old man could tell you so. It might not be supported by theory, but by heart and mind. He had once read that a historian working in a museum was thought of as another ancient piece in a forgotten collection, dust-covered and hidden away from the rest of the world.

Katic swore to change the stereotypical way of thinking. He, along with other museum curators now strove to not just display pieces, but to make them more interactive. Computers and technology had helped make that possibility a clearer reality. However, those leaps and bounds in technology created constant pressure to remain current and relevant, while showcasing history. The success of a program lives and dies at the hands of the historian handling the assignment. It came down to dedicated teams working on design and implementation, only after a board reviews and approves each step, before the step is taken.

Tedious and time consuming. The rewards did outweigh the labor taking place behind the scenes but, at times, it was mentally chaotic.

When Alexander Albright passed away, Katic could not help but reflect on his own immortality. More so, he questioned the size of the mark he'd leave on the world after he died. As a well-published author, a sought after public speaker, and a fine leader of the museum for nearly two decades, he knew he could not complain.

Katic had traveled the world. He explored uncharted corners of the globe. Involved in monumental digs then and the teams he had been a part of had unearthed countless treasures.

Countless treasures.

Sitting at his desk, but facing the windows behind, Katic stared at nothing in particular. It came down to time. It always came down to time. The question was quite simple, too. Did he want to continue on as a curator, working out of an office, stuck inside a building until he finally retired?

He was old now. Thin white hair covered his head. Even his trimmed beard was white. Solid abs hid behind a thickening pouch of fat he tried hiding when he bloused out his shirts after tucking them into his slacks. The added weight negatively impacted his knees and lower back. How long would it be before he needed a cane while walking? More importantly, how long before his health gradually deteriorated? He already had prescriptions for water pills, high blood pressure medication, and he was taking something for his cholesterol, too.

His phone rang, pulling him away from his thoughts. He spun his chair around and picked up the phone. "Dr. Katic," he said.

"It's Rosemary."

He'd seen her name and number on the phone ID. "You were right."

"He bought a plane ticket?"

"He bought five."

Katic leaned back in his chair. His degrees hung side by side against linen mats with medallion gold school seals, and were framed in matching chestnut wood. The corner hutch with glass doors and inside lighting showcased an array of awards in excellence, writing, and for discoveries.

His mark had been left on the world. And Rosemary, on the phone with him now, was all the proof he needed. "Five tickets? Quite interesting."

"Quite," she agreed. He could hear her fingers tapping away at a keyboard. "I went ahead and purchased first class tickets for us, as well, Father."

She insisted on calling him that. He never minded. It made him feel somewhat special. *Father*. What was not to like about such a profound title? "Perfect."

"I think we should discuss the details," she said.

"I couldn't agree more." He glanced at his wristwatch. "I won't be at the office much longer. I am sure your mother would be more than happy to set an extra place at the table tonight."

"Sounds good. I'll be over around seven," she said. "Should I let the rest of the team know about the trip?"

"Let's talk tonight. We can iron out the particulars. I want to hand pick who comes and who stays. In the meantime, I plan on reaching out to a few contacts I still have." He figured the list of people he knew would be worth contacting. He suspected Mr. Michael Albright may have contacted some of the same people.

"Of course," Rosemary said. "I'll see you around seven."

He was sometimes surprised at how involved Rosemary became with his past. She always loved his storytelling when she was growing up. His tales of adventure surely planted the seed within her imagination. The idea of the two of them going on an escapade together gave him a warm feeling. "Wonderful. I look forward to it."

The call ended.

Katic stood up and paced around his desk. He walked closer to the items presented inside the hutch. Each award meant something to him, triggered fond memories, but the call from his . . . daughter, from Rosemary —she was what always made his heart both race and melt.

He did not want to remain a curator until he retired. It was decided.

A curator position was fine, but he was not going to confine himself to the office, to this building, waiting for his last day of work. He wasn't too old to go back into the field.

He was going to recapture the part of him he'd lost, the part of him he'd . . . *retired.* He was an archaeologist first and foremost. Not meant for simple office staff.

Before him he saw a new chance for exploration and discovery. Adventure always awaited those willing to take the risk. Katic was ready for such an exploit!

The time, once again it was always about time, was now. Not to sound melodramatic, but now or never was completely applicable. Now, or succumb to boredom and humdrum and mediocracy.

Things were going to change. This was about more than adventure and riches. It was about setting the past right, about fixing a wrong allowed for far too long.

11

Fortaleza, Brazil

The SUVs drove through Fortaleza toward the North Atlantic Ocean. Crisp blue skies contained slim stripes of thin white clouds. Bright sunlight penetrated heavily tinted windows. The air conditioning inside the SUV blasted cold air from perfectly placed vents in both the front and back seats.

"The port warehouse is just ahead. Our helicopter is waiting for us there," Gregory Hanson explained. He drove fast, as if posted 50 km/h speed limit signs were merely a suggestion. Michael gripped the grab-handle above his door. It kept him from leaning too far left, or banging into the closed window on his right.

"They planning on leaving without us?" Marshall called out. Michael thought his skin looked a little green. He couldn't deny the sudden lefts and rights felt, at times, as if the SUV would roll over.

"They're not. They'll wait for us, don't worry about that. They're not going anywhere without us." Hanson looked into the rearview mirror, making eye contact with Marshall. "Thing is, storm fronts came down from the North Pacific and up from the south. Ecuador got hit overnight, the storm made landfall after eleven. Power outages reported all over the place. Southern Columbia is getting the brunt of the storm now."

"Won't be long before it reaches the Amazon," Natalie added.

Hanson nodded his head, grinning. "Exactly. I know you expect rain, and rain is something you'll get. Plenty of it. It's going to be a tropical storm over that rainforest. We don't need to get caught up in any high winds, or lightning, if you know what I mean."

Michael turned around. He made eye contact with Amber. "We're going to be okay."

She pursed her lips, not convinced.

"I, um—" Marshall started. "Do you know how many UKs and Irelands you can fit inside the Amazon Rainforest?"

"What?" Tymere said.

Michael understood. It was a diversion. He answered, "Five?"

Marshall shook his head. "Nope. Not even close."

"Ten?" Michael said.

"Let someone else guess," Marshall said. "Amber, if you combined the UK and Ireland into one, how many of them do you think fit into the Amazon?"

Amber shrugged. "Ten," she said, taking Michael's answer.

Hanson stopped the SUV in a parking lot. The ocean was on the left. Across from the lot was a small field with a paved square patch. On the patch sat a helicopter.

Amber closed her mouth. Her jaw muscles clenched. Michael saw her lower cheeks gyrate with little waves of tension.

"Seventeen," Marshall said. "You can fit seventeen of them inside the Amazon."

"That's . . . I don't even know what to say," Tymere said. He didn't bother trying to sound authentically impressed.

"Yeah. Actually, the Amazon touches nine different countries," Marshall added.

Hanson shut the engine. He unbuckled his seatbelt and twisted around. "Okay. We're going to cross the field to the chopper."

Amber was staring out the window at the helicopter. "Is that going to hold all of us?"

The black helicopter had four passenger windows on either side, the side door, and cockpit windshield. Four large rotor blades sat on top of the helicopter and the tail rotor was built into the end of the tail, and looked a lot like a giant house fan.

"All of us, and all of our gear." Hanson nodded toward the bird. "That is a H-One-Fifty-Five. Two turbine engines, it has one of the longest flight ranges, and is one of the faster cruising speeds when it comes to helicopters. Two-hundred-and-sixty-six kilometers. Which is around a hundred-and-sixty-five miles an hour. We can get about five hundred miles on a full tank."

"Is that far enough?" Tymere asked. "I was looking online last night."

"It's not far enough," Hanson said. "We have one fueling stop to make. Halfway. Then we should be all set."

"And it's safe, the helicopter? The pilot is good? I mean," Amber fumbled, "you know him? *You* trust him?"

Hanson said, "The pilot has over two thousand hours in that specific helicopter. He flew combat missions in Afghanistan, not in the exact same helicopter, but in a comparable one. I trust the pilot with my life. Especially in a storm. Dust storms in Afghanistan can happen at any time. Without warning. The pilot got everyone through safe and sound, every time."

"Okay," Amber said. "Okay, if you trust him."

"With my life." Hanson clapped his hands together. "Well? Why don't we gather our gear and head over."

They all grabbed backpacks and bags from the second SUV. Michael breathed in air that smelled of the salty sea, citrus, and coconuts.

"You met Neeson and Hamilton last night," Hanson waved a hand toward Chuck Neeson and Angelina Hamilton, who nodded a silent hello. The driver of the second SUV was the one pulling the gear out of the back of the vehicle. "Ford Reeves. He's our mechanic."

There was a round of hellos with handshakes.

Hanson added, "And I am not sure I mentioned it before, but Chuck here handles communications. Headsets. Walkies. Anything electronic. He speaks Portuguese as well. He can manage his way around many of the indigenous dialects and languages."

"How many different indigenous languages are there?" Natalie asked; she had one arm snaked around Tymere's arm.

Chuck Neeson gave a shrug, holding one large duffle bag by the straps with both hands. "There are, like, I don't know? Two-hundred-and-ten or seventeen different indigenous languages in the forest."

"Does that mean there are over two hundred different tribes of people?" Natalie asked. "Out there? In the rainforest."

"It does. And there are," Neeson said. "That's only of the two-hundred or so we know about. Some of the tribes might not be any bigger than thirty or forty people. But they have their own ways, their own customs, and so they also have their own language, or way of communicating."

"Hamilton takes care of weapons," Hanson said.

"Weapons?" Amber asked.

"Handguns, rifles. Things like that, mostly," Angelina Hamilton explained.

Michael didn't care for her usage of the word *mostly*. For now, he let it go. He knew they needed more than machetes for carving paths through thick jungle vines and dense foliage overgrowth. He wasn't positive the rest of the group was as aware of the need.

"We're about to encounter more than trees and rain when we step into that forest. Our job, under Hanson's direction, is to get you to your destination and back in one piece." Hamilton didn't flinch. She stood up tall, straight. "Once we reach the boat, we'll go over some survival protocols. It is going to be essential that we are all on the same page."

Hanson, once again, clapped his hands. "Okay, then. Let's get this stuff over to the helicopter and get this show on the road. I ran through the preflight checklist, and we're good to go."

Amber stopped walking. "Mr. Hanson—"

"Mister? Thought we were past that."

"Hanson, are you the pilot?" she asked.

He bowed some, a grand gesture, considering. "I am, and like I said, I trust me with my life."

In movies people ran toward helicopters bent forward so the rotor blades didn't decapitate them. The rotor blades on Hanson's bird were high enough off the ground that even if he jumped, Michael didn't think his hands could reach the blades.

Marshall sidled up alongside Michael. "Hey," he whispered. "I'm still filming. I hid the camera better."

"What?"

"Who is he to tell us we can't film on our own vacation?"

This wasn't exactly a vacation. "If he finds—"

"We good, gentlemen?" Hanson called out.

"We're good," Michael answered. Hanson wasn't really paying attention to them, though. Michael noticed, however, what held Hanson's attention. As they set the gear down by the belly of the helicopter, Michael turned left, toward the west. Above them might be a clear, crisp, blue sky. Where they were headed, it didn't look nearly as promising.

# # #

When the helicopter lifted off the ground, Michael gave Amber's hand a squeeze. It reassured him as much as it was meant to calm her. He saw Tymere and Natalie holding hands, as well. Natalie didn't look nervous at all. She had a big smile on her face. She kept looking at Tymere, and he couldn't seem to look away from his girlfriend. Michael found it all a little odd.

Marshall, who sat by a window, rested his forehead against the glass. While he attempted looking down at the ground as they ascended, his mouth was wide open in pure wonder.

Everyone inside the helicopter wore a headset with a microphone on a bendable arm.

"This is absolutely better than flying in a plane," Marshall exclaimed. The sound of his voice filled Michael's ears as if he were transmitting over a C.B. radio. "How high will we fly?"

"We're going to get up to around ten thousand feet. It is a perfect altitude for maximum cruising ability," Hanson responded. He sat in the pilot seat, the cyclic stick and throttle between his legs.

"Ten thousand feet. Wow," Marshall repeated. "Just a moment ago we were flying over houses. Like, residential track after residential track. And now all I can see is green. Everything is just . . . green."

Marshall was right. The canopy of the forest, a ceiling of giant green leaves, spread as far as the eye could see. There was no break in the leaves that Michael could see. Everything below those leaves was simply a mystery.

"That," Angelina Hamilton said, "would be the starting perimeter of the Amazon."

"No offense, Mike, but this is going to be like looking for a needle in a haystack."

Michael cringed. Hanson's team was hired to guide them through the jungle. He never explained what it was they were going after. Hanson had no idea why they were headed through the rainforest. They did not need everyone knowing they were searching for ruins and treasure.

Tymere let out a non-enthusiastic whoop. "Welcome to the jungle, people! Welcome to the jungle."

Far to the west, it was hard for Michael to miss the massing of dark clouds.

PART TWO

Two roads diverged in a wood, and I –
I took the one less traveled by.

Robert Frost

1

Terminal Hidroviário de Altamira - State of Pará, Brazil

After their third refuel, Hanson flew the helicopter into near-black clouds and heavy rain. The mood in the helicopter changed altogether before takeoff. Everyone noticed the ominous clouds to the west. There was no avoiding the weather.

The front Hanson had worried about earlier was on them. They had sped toward it, as if a welcome committee. Only the storm offered no appreciation in return.

"I don't like this," Amber said, reaching for Michael's hand.

Hanson answered. "It's just some rain. I haven't seen any lightning. This is a million dollar machine. No different than an airplane. The coast guard uses similar 'copters like this and fly them right into hurricanes to assist with rescue missions. You have nothing to worry about."

Michael was thankful Amber had shared her Dramamine with everyone. "Chew these. Don't swallow them," she had instructed.

Lightning flashed ahead of them. The white flash resembled a skeletal arm with too many fingers. The helicopter dropped.

Amber screamed. Michael wrapped an arm around her.

Hanson was no longer attempting to comfort Amber or the other passengers. He talked with Reeves, his co-pilot. The bird rose and dropped.

"Turbulence," Tymere said. "That's all it is."

"We just flew into a storm!" Amber argued.

"Can't we climb higher?" Marshall called out. He no longer looked thrilled about sitting so close to a window. He sat with his back straight and against his seat. He held his backpack on his lap and hugged it tight to his body. His complexion had gone ghost-white.

Hamilton, looking non-perplexed, held an electronic tablet in her hand. "Planes can. Helicopters can't. Planes are equipped to fly above storm clouds. They have pressurized cabins. We can't go that high—above storm clouds. But we do fly above some clouds. There are clouds as low as six-thousand feet. We're probably still around nine-thousand."

The helicopter surged, then dropped again.

Hamilton offered a half smile. "Eight."

"We're getting cross- and headwinds," Reeves pointed out. The wind picked up. It felt as if the helicopter was slowing down, despite ascending higher once again. The heavy rainfall made it difficult to see. Michael wondered how much visibility impaired Hanson's flying ability.

The helicopter spun around, as if now heading in the opposite direction. The sudden spin made Marshall groan. He hugged his backpack tighter.

Natalie sat rigid, still. She kept her eyes shut tight.

"I've got her," Reeves called out. "I've got her."

Michael saw Reeves pull back on the throttle. The helicopter climbed in the air toward a blackened sky. On the right, another bolt of lightning slashed across the darkness.

The sound of rain hammering the helicopter rang louder than the rotating blades and the helicopter engine combined. There was no air traffic control to provide direction or assistance. They were literally over an ocean of trees. Below, the rainforest canopy resembled waves frozen in time.

"We're not going to climb much higher," Hanson called out. "I need to maintain a visual of the surface."

So we don't fly into a mountain, Michael thought, *or into another low-flying aircraft*.

"With the humidity, and the rain, we don't want to risk icing," Hanson said.

Michael wished the pilot kept his thoughts to himself.

"Icing?" Amber said, her hand over the microphone.

"What?" Michael asked.

She removed her hand. "Icing?"

Michael heard her clearly in the headset. "We're staying low to avoid icing," Michael said, as if he understood everything going on. He wanted to convey confidence.

A third crash of lightning flashed directly in front of the helicopter.

"We took a hit," Reeves said. His tone of voice was calm.

"Roger," Hanson replied. "Engines?"

Reeves leaned forward. He tapped the dashboard displays. "We're good. Fully functioning."

Michael silently let out a sigh of relief. He squeezed Amber's hand. He didn't want to tell her everything would be okay, because everything he said, everyone else heard. He felt funny about sounding scared in front of the others.

"We're not far from the LZ," Hanson said.

How long had they been flying in the storm? It felt like hours. It may have been. Michael's stomach was tied in knots. He knew he wasn't breathing normally. He didn't think Natalie had opened her eyes once. Despite the seat harnesses, Tymere did his best to keep an arm around his girlfriend. His eyes were wide open. Michael wasn't sure if Tymere ever blinked.

Michael realized, now, Marshall had been praying. His prayers came across as whispers in everyone's ears. All at once, Michael thought all of his senses shifted. It felt as if the helicopter rotated upside down. The black clouds below them, the Amazon canopy above.

His stomach lurched up, or down. He wasn't sure. He was aware of bile in his throat. It burned.

Someone was screaming. Amber dug fingernails into the back of his hand.

Constant talk filled Michael's ears. Frantic speech. A slur of words. He wanted to rip off the headset. He couldn't let go of Amber's hand. Her fingertips gouged at his flesh.

They were not upside down. The helicopter was spinning out of control.

Tymere was shouting over and over: "Hang on!"

Michael saw Hanson wrestling with the cyclic stick, the throttle, and slamming his feet on pedals on the floorboard.

Hanson thrust the throttle forward. The helicopter reacted. The engines whined as they picked up speed and started toward the Amazon, getting far too close to the top of the jungle. However, the spinning stopped.

"Tail rotor in control," Reeves called out. "We fly low. Holding at three thousand. I think we're through the worst of it."

"We are," Hanson said. "Well done."

Well done? Michael realized he had been holding his breath.

He knew he had been once he started breathing again. It took him a moment to regain control of his chest and lungs. We're not going to die. We're *not* going to die.

2

The stormfront moved south. Michael relished the bluer sky ahead. As they cleared a path out of the wind and rain, the helicopter climbed higher and higher. Keeping the bird steady, Hanson gradually accelerated the cruising speed. Without turbulence, the rest of the trip was uneventful. Not that it mattered, the trauma was infused in Michael's soul by this point. Amber still hadn't said a word.

At least Natalie had her eyes open again. Marshall had not let go of the backpack, though. He looked arthritic. His fingers bent at odd angles, gripping the waterproof material at unnatural angles. Tymere's chest rose and fell rhythmically. He figured the both of them were still trying to regulate each breath, preventing full blown hyperventilation.

"Ladies and gentlemen, this is your captain speaking." Hanson's voice filled the headsets. Michael knew he was trying to be funny, sounding like a commercial airline pilot. He wasn't in a laughing mood. He didn't think he'd even be able to muster up a phony smile.

"With the passing of the storm, we are about ten minutes from our destination where, currently, we have gun metal grey skies, the humidity is close to one hundred percent, and there will be a constant chance of the rain returning. Please notice the seatbelt sign is still lit. So please refrain from unfastening your belts and moving about the cabin until after we have landed."

Michael hated admitting the rest of the flight went smoothly. He even caught himself looking out the window, admiring the view below. Fog, like morning mist, swam over the Amazon canopy.

Before long, the helicopter casually descended from the sky and zeroed in on a dirt lot beside the Serafim Delivery, a small business on the outskirts of the Brazilian warehouse district.

"That there is the Xingu River," Hanson explained. "It feeds into the Amazon. It is over sixteen hundred kilometers long, one of the largest clear water rivers within the Amazon. It passes over one-hundred-and-fifty miles, and spans twenty-two million acres of unspoiled rainforest."

As the helicopter set down, the rotation of the blades kicked up a whirlwind of dust. The spinning cloud hovered in place until Hanson was able to power down the helicopter engines.

"Now, I didn't do too badly at getting us here, did I?" Hanson said out loud, but clearly his personal pat-on-the-back was directed toward Amber. "Our vessel, *Seas the Day*, is docked right over there."

Michael followed where Hanson pointed. He wasn't sure what he expected. Unlike the black SUVs and the black helicopter, the two-tiered boat was all white. It looked like a fishing boat. They climbed out of the helicopter, and while everyone collected the gear, Michael asked: "What kind of boat is that?"

There were two boats docked side-by-side. They were similar in make and model. The closer of the two displayed *Seas the Day* along the side of the bow in bold black letters.

Hanson's team strapped holsters onto their waists. Each had a leg strap that fastened around the lower thigh. From a locked suitcase, they removed handguns and fit them into the holsters. They added extra ammo magazines into pouches along the hip of the holster.

Hanson stopped what he was doing, took his belt from Hamilton and, as he fastened it around his waist, and secured the belt around his thigh, he said: "*Seas the Day*? She's a two-thousand-two Wesmac. Thirty-eight foot. Dual fuel tanks. She's full and ready for the voyage. That, I can assure you."

"And are you the captain, as well?" Amber asked.

"Aye, I am." Hanson flashed her a smile. "Unless there are any more questions, I suggest we don't delay. Plenty of daylight left. We might as well begin this adventure. Michael has provided us with a destination, and if we head out now, we should be able to reach the specified area by dinner time."

"Dinner. Now you're talking," Marshall said. He wore his backpack on his back, and held a duffle bag by the straps in front of him. "And, may I ask, what is on the menu?"

Hanson laughed. "Whatever it is you guys catch while we navigate the river, Marshall."

"I'm all for fishing," Tymere said.

"You've never fished a day in your life, Ty," Natalie added.

Tymere rolled his eyes. "Like I said, I'm all for fishing, but what happens if we don't catch anything?"

"Prepared for everything, we have options on the boat."

They all started walking across the back lot toward the port. The river looked clear and calm, like glass. The humidity was thick. Like when he stepped out of the cool airport into the Brazilian sunlight, Michael felt beads of perspiration drip from under his arms immediately.

"What kind of fish can we expect to catch?" Marshall asked.

Hanson answered, "There is wolffish, peacock bass, pacu—"

"Pacu?" Natalie said. "Aren't pacu the same thing as piranha?"

"Piranha?" Amber said.

"No worries. The pacu are known as the vegetarian piranha. They are not meat eaters like their cousins." Hanson did not hide his amusement.

"So there aren't any piranha in that water?" Natalie asked.

"Oh, no. There are piranha in the water, as well. Both are quite tasty, I assure you," Hanson said. "But the piranha aren't the most dangerous species in the Xingu."

They were shuffling along toward the dock, trying to ignore the humidity, nearly entranced by the conversation. Michael realized Hanson was enjoying himself. He held the attention of everyone. Making them all feel uneasy seemed to make him happy.

"I'll bite," Marshall said. "What is the most dangerous species in the Xingu?"

Hanson glanced at each of the members of his team. "Would you guys agree it would have to be the anacondas?"

Hamilton, her hair in a braided ponytail, and a white tank top, nodded her head. "Definitely the anacondas."

Neeson, with one duffle bag slung over his shoulder and one clutched by the straps in his other hand, agreed. "Heard a fifty foot anaconda was spotted in the river a few years back."

Ford Reeves said, "The one from YouTube? Nah. Nah, man. That was disproved. It had to do with stretching the image on the video. They debugged that theory. There's no fifty foot anaconda out there."

"*Debugged?*" Hamilton asked.

"Yeah. They proved it wasn't true," Reeves said.

"Debunked. De. Bunked. Not debugged," Hamilton laughed.

"Debugged. Debunked. Same thing," Reeves said.

"Actually, it's not," Hamilton said. "One is correct, and one is a word you just made up."

"People say debugged," Reeves claimed.

"Who?" Neeson asked. "Who have you ever heard say the word debugged?"

"You knew what I meant, Angelina. Why do you always do that?" Reeves waved a hand about. "You never correct Chuck like that."

"We're here," Hanson said, ending the disagreement. He set down the gear he carried. He stepped off the wooden pier and onto the boat.

Up close, the fiberglass vessel looked immaculate. It most definitely was used for fishing. Michael had seen many similar boats for charter on Lake Ontario back home. A bunch of people rent the boat for three- to six- hours, and go out deep-lake fishing for the day.

Neeson handed over to Hanson the bags, then took the bags from Michael and his team. Hanson stacked everything neatly and then held out his hand. Natalie went first, climbing onto the boat.

"Welcome aboard," Hanson said.

He said this as each person crossed over the gap between the pier and onto the boat.

Hanson's team climbed aboard last, without Hanson's hand.

"Get comfortable. I am going to do a quick once-over and, before long, we'll be on our way." Hanson climbed up a small ladder and disappeared into the cabin; a moment later he stuck his head out. "Michael? Want to join me up here?"

Michael pointed at himself. Sometimes he had to remind himself this was his excursion. These guys worked for him. He was their employer. They had an air of authority about them, it made him feel a little self-conscious. "Yeah. Coming right up," he said. "Be right back," he told Amber. "You guys get situated."

"What can I do to help?" Tymere asked Hamilton as

Michael made his way up the ladder.

The main cabin, made of wood, had a large front windshield. The captain's chair was white leather. A bit worn, but solid and sturdy. The boat's wheel, polished chrome, was at the helm. There were a variety of electronics with lights flashing, and a CB radio mounted overhead. On the small table in the center of the cabin was a map with a geometry compass and grease pencils.

Hanson held a pencil in his hand and a sheet of paper. "These are the coordinates you provided." He pointed at the map. "We're here. We are going to travel the Xingu this way, through the Amazon, to about this point here. I am pretty sure we can dock the boat safely about here. Then it is going to come down to brute force as we cut a path through the jungle toward … here." He marked the map with a dark grease X.

Hanson stood up, hands on his hips. "That seem about right to you?"

"It does. Sounds perfect." Michael was both impressed, and anxious. Hanson never asked a single question about why they were headed into the jungle. The man didn't appear to have a curious bone in his body, and that was curious on its own. It didn't sit right with Michael. "Seems like a good plan."

"Right. Pretty direct path. We have some hills to climb. There is a ravine to cross. We keep an eye out for the wild animals," Hanson said, and then he laughed, "and the natives. There have been some reports of cannibalism around this region right … here. So we will keep a wide berth from that area altogether. Adds a little time to our journey, going up and around over here. But worth the extra steps. Wouldn't you agree?"

"Cannibals."

Hanson nodded, wearing a cocky smirk. "Yep."

"Definitely worth the extra steps going around them."

Hanson clapped his hands together. "That's what I thought. Okay. Then, if we are in agreement, I say let's get this party started."

3

Xingu River

Michael knew they were still in Brazil, but Xingu was completely different from the city they'd left that morning. The river was about seventy yards wide, from bank to bank, and thick with forest trees on the far bank. The trees were so dense he could barely see between the trunks. It reminded him of when he was a boy and in bed. When the closet door stood slightly ajar, he found himself always straining to see into the darkness. He was always positive something sinister was just out of sight, waiting to get him as soon as he fell asleep. The anxiety usually took over and he could remember screaming for his mom and dad. When they came rushing into the room, the room filling with light from the hallway, he remembered feeling foolish. Shame didn't stop him from asking them to close the closet door. They always would. Just to be safe, he remembered usually asking them to leave the bedroom door open a crack, too.

That was how he felt now, as if something sinister awaited them in the dense jungle beyond the frontline row of trees.

The small town they were in dotted the east bank with small, rundown businesses. There weren't many people around.

It looked like it might start raining again at any time. There was no sun to speak of. The overhead clouds were grey and black. Despite being by water, Michael thought he could smell the moisture in the air.

Chuck Neeson was at the stern of the boat, sitting on the edge beside a short pole with a white light on the end. "The funny thing about the natives, remember I mentioned there were over two hundred indigenous tribes in the forest? We don't know whether they've interacted with one another and, for all we know, there could be a hundred more tribes we aren't even aware of. The thing is, there are at least thirty-two tribes that have claimed stake to land in a perfect circle. Like the face of a clock," Neeson said.

"I don't—what's that mean?" Tymere enquired. Natalie was beside him. They sat together on the starboard side of the vessel.

Neeson pointed to a spot directly in front of him, and then to spots indicative of ticks on the face of a clock. "Let's say there is a tribe here at twelve o'clock. Then another, here, at one, and two, and three, and so on."

"But there are only twelve points on a clock," Marshall said.

"True. However, in that jungle," Neeson pointed toward the forest across from the port side of the boat, "there is more than one clock. Reminds me of those crop circles you always see on the news. The tribes are all set up in perfect circles, with a tribe located at the five minute marks on a clock. And there is always one at the center of the circle. I'm telling you, it's a little bizarre."

"How can that be?" Amber asked. "I thought the Amazon canopy was so complete that the ground of the forest never sees sunlight?"

Hamilton laughed. "You've done some homework, I see."

"That is also true," Neeson said. "Researchers used LiDAR to—"

"LiDAR?" Michael interrupted. "What's that?"

"Light detection and ranging. See what it does is, it examines the surface of the earth using light pulses. The pulses bounce off whatever is below and then can generate three-dimensional, precise topographical images—stripping away things like tree leaves, and even trees, to see what is beneath it all," Neeson said. "It gave the researchers a clean look at the geology of it all."

The boat engines came to life, revving.

Reeves removed the moorings from the dock, then stepped back onto the boat as it glided away from the pier. "Here we go. How about some fishing?"

Before long, Michael and his friends had poles in hand, lines cast. Trolling the Xingu, they smiled, looking at one another.

"This is kind of nice," Natalie said. "Relaxing."

Hanson's team didn't fish. They worked, moving supplies around, taking them off the deck and down into the lower cabin.

Tymere said, "I mean, this ain't terrible."

Natalie lurched forward.

"You got a bite!" Tymere shifted his weight. He wrapped an arm around Natalie's waist. "What do we do? What does she do?"

"Don't pull back on the line yet," Hamilton instructed. "Wait for it. Wait. Now! Yank back hard with the pole."

Natalie reacted.

Hamilton yelled, "Fish on! Okay. Now keep the line taut!"

"Taut?" Natalie called out. "How?"

"Let out a little line. Just a little. The fish will struggle and wear itself out," Hamilton instructed. She moved about the deck and now stood behind Natalie. "It's a big one. Could be a catfish, or peacock bass! Now, keep the pole straight. Raise the tip of the pole! Don't try to overpower the fish. It will release too much line, or snap it. We don't want the line to snap!"

"How do I reel it in, then?" she asked.

"Move aside, move!" Hamilton cleared a path so Natalie could walk around the deck, keeping her fishing rod straight. "Someone grab the net!"

Tymere retrieved the net from the side of the deck. "I got it!"

"Crank the reel. Start bringing in the line a little at a time," Hamilton explained.

Michael had an arm around Amber, watching everything unfold.

He turned, checking on how Marshall was doing. He saw Marshall's line go tight, and the end of the pole bent forward. All at once, Marshall was pulled toward the back end of the boat. Marshall lost his footing.

"Marshall!" Michael called out, dropping his own fishing pole and lurching toward his friend.

He was too slow.

Marshall stumbled forward and fell over the side of the boat and into the river. His body made a big splash as he went under the water. Did he have a life jacket on? None of them did! They should have put on life jackets! Were there even life jackets on the boat? Hanson never said. Michael had never thought to ask.

"Stop the boat," Michael screamed. "Hanson! Stop the boat!"

Natalie spun around.

"Don't let go," Hamilton shouted, reaching for Natalie's fishing pole.

Tymere rummaged through his backpack. He grabbed a Bowie knife and tucked it into his waistband. Next, he lifted a bench along the cabin and snatched up a life jacket. He put it on and, without snapping the fasteners together, leapt over the side of the boat and into the water.

Marshall still hadn't surfaced.

"Hanson!"

The engines stopped. The current had them. They continued forward. The engines came on again, the boat slowed, and then slowly started going backwards. Hanson must have switched the engines into reverse.

Tymere bobbed on the water. "I don't see him!"

Amber pointed. "There he is!"

Something wet, thick, and black was wrapped around Marshall's neck.

"It's an anaconda," Reeves said. "He hooked a freaking snake!"

Hamilton looked down at the taut line on Natalie's pole, as if reeling in the fish was more important than the man being drowned by a river monster. "Dammit," she muttered, and dropped the pole while reaching for her sidearm.

"You can't shoot!" Michael said, raising an arm to block her view. "You might hit Marshall!"

Natalie screamed for Tymere to swim for the boat.

Amber found an orange life ring. It was tethered to the deck. She flung it out onto the water toward Tymere.

The snake extended its tail end, and re-gripped its hold on Marshall. His arms flailed for a moment. He didn't make a sound, though. The snake was wound tight around his neck. Instead of splashing, Marshall's hands worked uselessly at pulling the snake away from his throat. The giant creature pulled him under again as Tymere reached them.

Tymere removed his life vest. His hand went underwater for a moment. When it came back up, he held an unsheathed knife. It was the Bowie Michael had purchased for them. Tymere fit the blunt end, with the saw, between his teeth, cupped his hands together, and then dove under.

"No!" Natalie screamed.

Michael felt useless. Lost. There was nothing he could do.

Reeves had a long wooden boat hook; he thrust the hook end into the water. "Where did they go?"

How long have they been underwater? Michael stood on the edge of the deck, about to jump into the water. "I don't see them!"

Neeson grabbed him by the arm, holding him back. "We don't need to try rescuing three people. That would only serve to make matters worse. Stay in the boat!"

"But—"

"Stay in the boat!" Neeson was not messing around. He tugged on Michael's arm, pulling him down from off the edge of the boat.

The water churned, as if being brought to a boil. "There! There they are!" Michael pointed.

Hanson brought the boat around.

Tymere popped up to the surface. He held a section of snake in one hand, and with the other he stabbed the knife through the anaconda's flesh. When the knife came free, he stabbed it a second time. This time, he sliced downward, creating a gaping gash along the side.

Reeves jabbed the end of the hook into the water.

Marshall's hand shot up and out of the water. His fingers grabbed ahold of the end of the boat hook.

Tymere swam over to Marshall, pulling him up and under his arm.

"Hang on, buddy," Tymere kept saying.

Reeves pulled with all of his might. Hamilton got behind him, wrapping her arms around his waist. Together, they attempted getting the men out of the water. Tymere lost his grip and went under.

Amber, on her knees, leaned over the edge of the boat with an arm extended. "Tymere!"

Tymere's head emerged from the water. He shook water out of his eyes and mouth. His other arm still had Marshall under the arm.

Michael couldn't see the snake. He couldn't believe Tymere had managed to slash it with a blade. He had never witnessed anything as crazy, or heroic, in person before. "Get them back into the boat!"

Natalie grabbed hold of the rope for the life ring. Hand over hand, she brought the preserver back to the boat. She lifted it out of the water. Taking aim, she tossed it toward Tymere.

Tymere was able to hook an arm through the ring.

Reeves and Hamilton took the end of the rope from Natalie and started reeling them in.

As the two got closer to the boat, Michael hooked the other end of the ring with his arm, and then took hold of Tymere.

The group, gathered on the aft side of the boat, hoisted first Marshall, and then Tymere out of the water.

"Marshall's not breathing!" Natalie yelled.

Tymere, lying on his back, coughed up river water. He pushed up onto a forearm and then rolled over onto his stomach. Propped up on his arms, he coughed up even more water.

Marshall wasn't moving. The area around his neck was red, bruising.

Amber pushed everyone out of the way and knelt at Marshall's side. She planted the heel of her hand on Marshall's chest. "Mike, when I say blow, give Marshall two strong breaths into his mouth."

She began CPR, pressing her weight onto her arms. Marshall's chest depressed with each thrust downward. She counted off compressions. At twenty, she stopped. "Blow."

Michael, who had tipped Marshall's head back and pinched his nose closed, covered Marshall's mouth with his own. He blew into Marshall's mouth twice. Marshall's chest rose with each breath.

Amber restarted compressions. Wisps of her hair hung down, stuck against her face. She ignored the hair in her eyes. She concentrated on counting off each compression. When she stopped, she said, "Now."

Michael did as instructed.

This time, Marshall's body arched. His face wrinkled, and he spit up water.

"Turn him on his side," Amber instructed.

"He's breathing." Natalie smiled, but she was crying. She was bent over Tymere. "He's breathing."

Marshall's body heaved and writhed. More water sputtered out of his mouth and nose. He began coughing. When he opened his eyes, they went wide in panic. His hands shot to his throat. "Get it off me! Get it off!"

"You're okay now, Marshall. You're alright." Amber placed her hands on his arm in an attempt at calming him.

Marshall sat up. His hands were still on his neck, tracing it across to his shoulders. "What happened?" He didn't wait for an answer. "It had me. It was pulling me under. It was so strong. It kept squeezing me. I mean, squeezing me. I thought I was dead for sure," he said.

"You were," Tymere said. He was dripping wet and kept sliding the back of his hand over his forehead.

Marshall swallowed. "I what?"

"You were gone," Tymere said.

"Amber brought you back," Natalie said. "Tymere jumped into the water and pulled you out. That was so foolish!"

"Yes, it was," Hanson said.

"I had to do something," Tymere said. "That thing was big. I mean, that thing was freaking huge. It was a monster."

"It sure was a monster," Hanson agreed. "Rescuing one person in this river is dangerous enough. You increased the odds of death tenfold when you jumped in after him."

Michael detected a sneer in Hanson's tone of voice when he said, *him*.

"Well, it's like I said, I had to do something," Tymere said.

Ignoring Hanson, Natalie continued, "And then Amber did CPR. You weren't breathing."

Marshall's breathing slowed. Long, deep breaths. "Oh my God."

Hanson stood over them. "You gave us quite a fright."

"Tymere? Amber?" Marshall said. "I don't think I can ever thank either of you enough."

"It's what friends do," Tymere said.

Michael saw a look in Marshall's expression. Was Marshall wondering, if the roles were reversed, if he would have jumped into a river to save Tymere? What Tymere had done was heroic. Michael realized he had not dived into the river, either. Amber had held him back, but if she wasn't there to stop him, would he have actually dived in?

If any of his friends were in danger, was he going to be man enough to save them, even if it meant at the risk of his own life?

He liked to think he would. The truth was, he wouldn't know until thrust into such a situation. One fact was certain, Tymere would, and without hesitation.

Marshall had *given them quite a fright, which was an understatement*, Michael thought. Michael whispered. "Hey, we can turn around, man. We can end this right now and head back. What happened was out of control. I wanted you to know. We can head back home and forget the rest of this trip."

Marshall was quiet for a moment. Michael knew he was giving the idea of returning to the States serious consideration.

"I'm telling you," Michael added, "there would be no hard feelings. And it wouldn't hurt stopping at a hospital just to have you—"

"No." Marshall held up a hand. He made eye contact with Michael. Water dripped from his hair into his eyes. "I want to keep going. That was the scariest thing that has ever happened to me. I could have died."

"Yes, you could have."

"If we turn around now, then it was kind of for nothing. I want to see this through, Mikey. I don't want to give up now."

"It's not giving up if we go home. It's not."

"It would be to me. And I, for one, do not want to quit. I am committed to this. I want to . . . you know, find what we came out here to find."

Michael was thankful Marshall hadn't mentioned treasure. He didn't need Hanson or any of his team catching wind of why they were out here. They'd find out eventually, of course. For now, he liked keeping that part of the expedition under wraps.

"You're sure?"

"I'm positive."

Michael clapped Marshall on the back. "That was scary as hell, man."

Marshall grinned. "Right?"

Michael addressed his friends. "Maybe we should all wear life vests from this point on."

A life vest wouldn't stop an anaconda from dragging someone under water, Michael knew. It seemed like having some kind of plan at this point seemed important. If anything, it made him feel as if he had some control.

"We have plenty for everyone," Hanson said. He waved a

hand.

Hamilton lifted a bench seat. She removed life vests from storage and passed them out. "It's not a bad idea."

Above, thunder rolled. Dark clouds moved across the already greying sky. Despite being early evening, the sun was gone and nighttime came early.

"I am going to get back to steering the boat," Hanson said. "Reeves, Neeson. Why don't the two of you handle catching us some dinner?"

Amber whispered near Michael, "Can we trust these people, or what?"

He didn't have an answer. "We have to," he said.

"Do we? Because when Marshall fell into the water, if Tymere didn't jump in to save him, I don't think any of them were planning on helping," she said. "I am getting a bad feeling about them. They make me uneasy."

They made Michael feel uneasy, as well. He wasn't ready to admit as much. Not yet. They would spend a few days in the jungle, find the treasure, and head for home in no time at all.

4

As the boat moved down the river, Michael suddenly became aware of the sounds around them. He wished he was better educated when it came to birds. The songs echoed through the trees lining the banks, and seemed to bounce off the water. The chirping made it near impossible to tell from what direction the sounds came. He saw different types of birds, all of various colors, fly overhead. Some sat on the water, like ducks. He heard insects joining the ballad. They might have been louder than the birds. Their insect song was more *constant* and insistent. High-pitched music of hind legs rubbing together. A chorus to rival the string section of any orchestra, to be sure. Together, the harmony of it all was quite soothing.

There were other animals amid the trees, calling out in communication with others of their breed. Michael had no idea what type of animals sounded that way. Monkeys?

"Are there monkeys in the forest?" Michael asked.

Hamilton grinned. "There are howlers, spider monkeys, capuchin, squirrel, tamarins, and marmosets."

"Marmosets?" Amber asked. "Aren't they, like, palm sized?"

"They weigh in around four ounces. They have claws, not fingers, like other primates. And they're not too bright, the way most people think monkeys can be," she said. "The tamarins aren't much bigger. About the size of a squirrel. They have faces that look like Dr. Seuss' Lorax."

"Are they dangerous?" Natalie asked.

"The monkeys? They're vocal. The squirrel monkeys live in clans by the hundreds. They talk back and forth all day long. But dangerous? I'm not aware of any dangerous monkeys in the rainforest."

Reeves and Neeson had reeled in five catfish. They were excited about the catches. Michael and his friends watched without comment. The mood on the boat had shifted since

Marshall fell in. Hamilton filleted the fish, cutting from the head, at the backbone down to the tail, and then sliced the meat free from the skin with ease and skill while Neeson fired up a tabletop propane grill.

"No baboons?" Marshall asked, listening to the exchange.

Hanson grinned. "You're thinking of Africa. No, there are no baboons in these parts."

Small miracles, Michael thought. He couldn't shake the images in his mind of the anaconda snaking around Marshall's neck, pulling him underwater.

"I figure by the time we finish our meal, we should be looking for a place to dock," Hanson said.

"We're almost there?" Amber asked.

Hanson stared at the trees along the bank. He almost looked lost in thought. But he turned around, slowly. "We are almost there. It's definitely getting late. I might suggest we spend the evening on the boat. Get a good night's sleep, and then start out in the morning."

Michael didn't want to delay trekking through the forest. They had a long journey on foot ahead of them. However, Hanson had a point. It didn't make sense leaving the boat and immediately setting up a shelter for the night. The idea of camping in the middle of the Amazon held very little appeal. Sleeping out in the open of such a dangerous environment was the biggest downfall of their adventure, as far as he was concerned. "I'd agree. That makes the most sense."

And the darkness fell around them.

5

Rosemary Katic wore her long, brown hair braided under her green baseball cap. The bill shaded her otherwise bright blue eyes. Her short sleeve shirt and loose fitting khakis felt like too much clothing in the Amazon humidity. The heavy rains brought no relief, but thankfully she'd remained dry.

She and Father hid inside the empty warehouse and watched as Hanson and his team led Albright and his friends to the vessel docked beside the one they would use for following. She watched until the boat pulled away from the bank and began making its way down the river. The motors churned the near-brown water, leaving a short trail of frenzied white froth with bubbles, and a reverse V wake that shimmied outward toward both the west and east banks.

"They've gone," she said.

Nicholas Katic paced back and forth. In the center of the warehouse stood two picnic tables. On the tables were their gear, packed in duffle bags. Nicholas wore tan pants and a French blue shirt. His fishing vest was littered with pockets, each stuffed with items he said he couldn't travel without. "We will give them an hour's head start, maybe two. That should be plenty."

Rosemary wasn't as comfortable with the plan as she had been a few weeks ago. She understood the dynamic between Father and Alexander Albright, but wasn't convinced the ends justified the means. She'd heard plenty of stories, from the time she was a little girl, about how Alexander was the reason her family suffered so much pain and loss. She believed part of any found treasure was owed to the Katic family, but wasn't positive Father's plan was the right course of action.

Not anymore.

She didn't consider Father a ruined man. He received multiple college degrees and held an esteemed position with a prestigious museum. It wasn't that life had been difficult for the

Katics, but that didn't mean life couldn't have been different.

It was easy getting caught up with Father in all of his excitement. His emotions about the past were part of his personality. His passion for history made him who he was. It wasn't the death of Albright that got him wound up, but the idea for a chance to go on another adventure.

The adventure was oftentimes more exhilarating than the find. That was something he'd always said. She believed it. The journey is where character is discovered, and honed, it was where fears were found and faced.

Rosemary knew this was as much about the adventure as it was treasure. There would be some glory, and fame thrown in, as well. A discovery like the one they now searched for would generate media and university interests globally.

She only wished Father owned the pirate's map, and they led the expedition rather than be stuck in a maddening game of cat and mouse, especially when the mouse had zero idea there was a game afoot.

This particular adventure, it turned out, was just Rosemary, Father, and two guides, who were secretly pursuing Michael Albright and his friends.

Seeing Michael and the others forced her to second guess the entire plan, which was not good. Not now, especially. She knew she needed to be all in. After all, they were about to venture out into the wild jungle of the Amazon Rainforest. It made her feel somewhat mentally unprepared.

"Father," she said. It was better to broach the topic now. They hadn't reached a point of no return, just yet. He may think so, but she thought maybe she could convince him otherwise. Turn around, head home. That made more sense.

"We're about ready. Anything else you think we'll need?" Nicholas unzipped a duffle bag. He rummaged through the contents. He wore a grin she was not used to seeing. Father looked happy.

He needed this. She supposed she did, as well. She knew she shouldn't let cold feet interfere with something the two of them had planned from the day she'd been old enough to hold an intelligent conversation.

Closure. Vengeance?

He needed this! She needed this!

"No, I think we're good. I believe we have everything we need." Rosemary walked toward him. "I was just thinking about, you know, what it is we plan on doing."

Nicholas gently clasped his hands on Rosemary's shoulders. He looked into her eyes. "You have no idea how proud I am of you. But it is more than that. I never dreamed I would actually get the chance to do something like this with you. I mean, you and I, in Brazil, going after buried pirate treasure? How exciting is that? How amazing is this?"

This wasn't going to be easy, she realized. "This is very exciting."

"I only wish your mother was a little healthier. I really think she wanted to join us. Didn't you get the impression she wanted to come with us on the hunt?" he asked.

Rosemary didn't think her mother wanted any part of this. The dinner they all had had a few weeks back consisted of her and Father sitting close, talking about the trip, and taking notes. Not once did her own mother ever express any interest. In fact, she had looked bored, and maybe annoyed with the conversation. And maybe a little mad as the plan unfolded before her?

"I think she would have loved coming along. You know, if she was feeling better."

He nodded in agreement. "What were you going to say?"

"Hmm? Oh, before? I was just, I—"

"What is it, honey?"

"What if we try calling Michael Albright?"

"Calling him?" Nicholas pointed toward the closed warehouse door. "Dear—"

"I was wondering if trying to join his team might be the better approach to this?" She shrugged, as if the idea had come to her. "We can share ... everything?"

"The plan is simple. We've—"

"I know the plan. I understand what we're doing, and how we're going to get things done." It didn't sit right with her.

"It's not as if we are stealing anything. We're going to *right* a long overdue wrong." He folded his hands together in front of him. The way he stood, feet close together, made him resemble every bit the curator of a museum. The very non-threatening pose gave off an air of peace and tranquility. Nothing about the stance indicated the turning wheel and grinding gears turning inside his head. "Not to mention, we have no idea what Michael's intentions are."

"I am sure he would sell the discovery to the museum, if you made an acceptable offer." She suspected, for Albright, this was as much about paying homage to his recently deceased father as it might have been about thrill-seeking.

"My museum? How can you be so sure? Why wouldn't he and his friends keep the treasure for themselves? They would be entitled to keep it. No one could even fault them for keeping some box of gold from hundreds of years ago," he said.

"I can't say for sure what his intentions would be—"

"And therein lies the problem, dear."

6

Michael stood on the port side of the vessel. He could not take his eyes off the trees. Occasionally, he looked up at the darkening sky.

Amber walked over. She took his hand. "What are you thinking about?"

"I was thinking how much I wish my father was still alive." He continued looking straight ahead. He didn't think by saying such a thing out loud it would hit him like this. He wouldn't cry, but the sudden tightening of his chest and the slight constricting of his throat was unexpected.

Amber wrapped an arm through his.

"It's more that I wish he were here, leading this expedition," he said. It was true. Although he appreciated all his father had accomplished, he knew he could have taken more interest in all of the stories. "How cool would it have been to take trips like this with him? The two of us digging up treasures? You know, like, father and son treasure hunters."

"That would have been cool," Amber said. "Didn't the two of you ever go exploring when he …"

"Was still alive?" Michael finished her sentence. "You see, that's the thing, we didn't."

"Maybe he just—"

"No. Not him. Me." Michael tapped his chest. He then waved a hand toward the forest. "Even though my dad stopped going on expeditions like this just before I was born, he still held on to this *fire* for history, and archaeology, and let's face it … finding buried treasures. And whenever I went into his office—you've seen his office?"

"A hoarder if I ever met one," Amber laughed. Michael knew she teased, but also her assessment was nothing short of quite honest.

"Exactly. The thing about all of that clutter, though, is my father could tie some exotic, dangerous, nearly unbelievable story to every single item in his office. The magical wooden staff, the golden clay pot, the Bengal jewel . . . there isn't a single thing in his office that wasn't tied to an amazing adventure," Michael said. He stood with both hands on the rail. His grip was too tight. His knuckles were turning white.

Amber held his arms in both of her hands. "How lucky you were to share in the stories."

Michael knew tears brimmed and he tried blinking them back. "That's the thing, I should have been lucky. He, my—my dad always invited me to sit down and talk, you know? Sit and talk. He'd often try striking up a conversation with me by picking up one of his objects and saying something like, 'Did I ever tell you, Mikey, how I had to deep sea dive during a brewing storm on the South Pacific in order to recover this … whatever it was … from some sunken ship or submarine?'"

"You don't remember what it was? Or what kind of ship was sunk?" Amber asked.

"Now you get it," Michael said.

"No, I don't."

"He always wanted to bring me into his past. Share it with me. But I—I never had the time for him. Not then. I was too worried about video games, or hanging out with my friends. Do you know what I did? I brushed him off. I barely listened to a word he said, but I especially didn't pay attention when he started reminiscing, the stories of his glory days. I was a horrible son." Michael used his thumb to wipe under his eyes. There was no hiding his sadness, his pain. Not at this point.

"Mike, we all do the same thing to our parents. You don't think I've never slammed my bedroom door while my mother was in mid-sentence? Or turned on earbuds and listened to music during family dinners? I ignored my parents. And I will bet you Tymere and Marshall and Natalie all ignored their parents, too." Amber had pressed in close. She still held onto his arm, but she angled herself so she could look up and into his eyes.

Michael sometimes couldn't believe how fortunate he was. Amber was an amazing lady. Beautiful. The best part was, for whatever reason, she actually loved him. He couldn't figure out why. He wouldn't ever tempt fate by asking, either. "I know. I know most kids ignore most parents. I wish I knew now what I didn't know then, you know?"

"I do. It's simply called regret."

"And I regret taking my father for granted. If I could get back some of that time, a fraction of it, I would spend all of that time sitting in a chair across from him in his office and let him tell me story after story. I would."

Amber smiled. "I know you would."

"I was thinking about something." Tymere appeared on the other side of Michael. The sound of his voice broke the moment, for which Michael was thankful.

"Yes?"

"I'm picturing our point of entry into the forest," Tymere said.

"What about it?"

"The pirate," he said.

"Roche Braziliano?"

"Yes. I didn't see it before, see the details. But you said he was from Bahia, Brazil, right, before he became a buccaneer out of Port Royal in Jamaica?" Tymere recapped.

"True."

"Well, on a map, Bahia is like the far east, and kind of to the south in Brazil."

"It is."

"And Jamaica is way north. How did it come to be that Roche decided to bury his treasure so far from . . . anything? I mean, the Xingu River is about as far west of Brazil as we can go. We're talking, like, a thousand miles or more."

"Or more. Most certainly. You see, the limited information historians have on Roche say that he was an explorer. And one of his favorite pastimes was traveling the different rivers and venturing deep into the Amazon," Michael explained.

"So he stumbled on the ruins?"

"He stumbled on the ruins and, from what my father could figure out, decided that it would be the perfect place to hide his wealth before leaving for Jamaica," Michael said. "I guess he figured if he were the first to discover the ruins in, however many hundreds of years, then he could assume no one else would come across them accidentally, and even if someone did, his treasure, we shall assume, was so well hidden within, he wasn't worried about discovery."

Tymere pointed at the trees along the bank. "And the map—"

"The map will lead us both to the ruins, and to the treasure," Michael said. *I think,* he thought.

"Which leads me to my next question. How do we know Roche didn't return for his treasure *before* going to Jamaica, or sometime before he was sent to Spain to stand trial?"

"Well." Michael shrugged. "We don't. Not really."

Tymere looked deflated.

Michael put a hand on Tymere's shoulder. "What difference does it make? Don't you see, we are on the adventure of a lifetime. We might not find a damn thing, but that doesn't matter. Look where we are! Think about what we are about to do."

"Worse case," Tymere tried, "we find the ruins."

Michael cocked his head to one side. "That's true. Worse case."

"There it is," Hanson pointed. "We've made it, with barely a scratch."

With barely a scratch. Hanson thought he was funny. Marshall had almost died, and Tymere could have drowned. There was nothing funny about Hanson's comment. Michael resented it. He was beginning to resent Hanson and his entire team.

It started raining. The drops pelted the river; for a moment Michael watched the ripples where the boat's spotlight captured a ring of the water.

Hanson brought the boat up to the bank. Reeves hopped out and secured the vessel to a fallen tree. Hanson's cell phone rang. Michael watched him as he answered it. He wished he could hear the conversation. The call lasted all of thirty seconds before Hanson ended the call and replaced his phone into one of his vest pockets.

"We get cell service out here?" Marshall asked. "Thought we would need, like, a satellite phone or something."

Hanson laughed. "Believe it or not, there are makeshift towers around. Can't promise you'll always have bars. For the most part, we should get service. At least along the edge of the forest. Once we're a few days into the Amazon, who knows?"

Tymere said, "Strategic cell towers were placed inside the

rainforest. They're solar powered and only give a two point five mile radius. So, like our captain said, service might be spotty, but there is service where we are headed."

Michael never ceased to be surprised by Tymere's knowledge. It wasn't that he knew everything, but he sure seemed to know a bit about a lot of things.

"We're going to sleep here tonight. On the boat. Tomorrow," he waved at the forest, "we will begin the hike. I suggest finding a dry spot, and getting some sleep."

Darkness surrounded them once Hanson switched off the spotlight.

"Why did you do that?" Marshall asked.

"The light? It attracts mosquitoes. We're not talking gnat-sized mosquitoes like you see in New York. The insects here are the size of birds. Trust me. You don't want them sucking your blood while you sleep. There is netting below deck. Get under it and, like I said, get some sleep."

Bird-sized mosquitoes, Michael thought. *Peachy*.

7

Amazon Rainforest

The sound of birds singing and monkeys bickering woke Michael. Amber was curled up beside him under the netting. He slowly lifted himself onto an arm. Looking around, he saw his friends sleeping soundly around the small cabin. Michael knew Hanson and his crew set up nets in the main cabin, where they would be better able to keep Michael and his friends safer.

Michael was surprised by two things; one, that he actually fell asleep, and two, that he slept soundly. He guessed he had been mentally drained. A lot happened yesterday. Aside from all the travel by helicopter, it was the unfortunate mishap from cruising down the river.

This was the first moment where Michael began to have regrets about the expedition. He laid his head back down and listened to the steady breaths of Amber sleeping. She looked peaceful, and beautiful. The regret stemmed from there. His father was a professional. The man had dedicated his life to this kind of journey. He was smart, educated, and prepared. He knew what he had been doing. Was taking his best friends on such a dangerous mission as stupid as it now sounded?

He heard footsteps from above. Boots on the thin floor sounded like a marching army inside the boat's hull. It seemed Hanson and his team were waking, as well.

Regrets aside, another part of Michael felt wound up. A surge of energy passed through his body. He could feel a tingling in his fingers and toes. It was clearly adrenaline. He opened and closed his fists, savoring the sensation. Ready or not, they were about to enter the Amazon, they were about to hunt for ancient ruins and a hidden chest filled with treasure. There was something very Robert Louis Stevenson about the entirety of it all.

Breakfast was grilled fish.

Hanson cut open a dark, yellowish ball. Inside was a juicy, seed-filled center. "This is maracuya. It is a passion fruit. Dig out the juice and the seeds. You can eat both. Not the rind. That part wouldn't taste good anyway."

"We can eat the seeds?" Marshall asked.

Using a spoon, Hanson scooped a chunk of the fruit into his mouth. Seeds and all. After chewing, he said, "You can. The maracuya has plenty of vitamins, and fiber. It grows wild from a flower on vines inside the forest. There are other fruits safe for eating in the jungle, like the aguaje, cupuacu—which is like a mango, and the acai. The acai look like grapes. They are tiny purple berries. High in vitamin C. I will point out these, and more, as we make our way into the jungle over the next few days. We will forage for food along the way. Less supplies to carry that way."

For the most part, everyone ate in silence. Michael took the time to contemplate the moment. This was it. The time was now. In a few minutes they would leave the safety of the boat and venture out into the wild. The untamed wild. It was a frightening thought, and suddenly all too real.

"Looks like we've received a blessing for the day," Hanson said. "Only a few clouds and the sun is out."

It was, indeed, a beautiful morning. Although the sun reflected off the Xingu River, only rays of light penetrated the forest canopy. Beyond the trees it was still dark. Michael tried not to take that as an omen, as foreboding as it might look.

When breakfast ended, the life of the two groups returned in anxious chatter. They collected their gear. Hanson and his team wore black tactical pants, black t-shirts, and black boots. They had a very Tomb Raider look. Michael felt quite cliché. He had purchased khaki pants, going for more of an Indiana Jones style.

"I wasn't too sure about these costumes," Natalie said. She pulled on the backpack straps. "But I'm kind of digging it. How do I look, Ty?"

"Stunning. As usual," he said.

The backpacks were heavier than expected. There was a first aid kit in each. Rope. Bug spray. They each had a machete, and an expensive Bowie knife. Tymere's knife bordered on something legendary.

"We should consider naming yours," Marshall said.

Tymere wrinkled his brow. "What?"

"Your knife. It deserves a name. Knights would often name their swords depending on what happened during a battle, or how the steel was forged. After what you did with your knife, I was thinking it kind of deserves a name."

Tymere laughed. "I'll tell you what? You come up with one, and we can hold a ceremony or something."

"All right. I'll do that."

Affixing the sheaths onto their belts, they looked like genuine adventurers, Michael thought. *Looked*, being the key word.

Michael was doing little more than role playing, he knew. Pretending to be some kind of leader. His friends looked to him for guidance, why? Because he paid for everything? Because this trek was his idea?

He wasn't his father. Would his entire . . . sham be exposed? Was he needlessly putting everyone's life in danger?

If it wasn't such a serious moment, he would have laughed. What in the world were they doing here? What in the hell were they about to do?

Michael knew he was not his father! Would Alexander approve of any of this? He doubted it.

He was filled with doubt, once again.

Michael shut his eyes tight. He gave his head a little shake. Short, but fierce. He tried pushing away negative thoughts. He knew they could hinder the success of the trip.

"Hey," Amber tugged on his arm. "You okay?"

Michael opened his eyes. He tried smiling. "I'm just, I guess, a bit apprehensive. If I am being honest."

"I think we all are," she said. "But you know what? This is pretty exciting. I mean, look where we are. Look what we're about to do. This is the craziest thing I have ever done, the most reckless, but I have never felt more alive!"

He felt it, as well. The life. The exhilaration of it all.

Hanson clapped his hands together. "Well? Are we ready? Daylight is burning, and we want to get as many miles in as we can before finding a place to bunk down for the night."

It was barely seven in the morning, and Hanson was talking about bunking down for the night already. Michael figured it was the day's only real goal. Since they wouldn't reach the ruins for at least two full days of hiking, getting from point A to point B and then finding a safe place for the night was the objective.

"Let's do this," Michael said.

8

Thwack! Thwack! Thwack!

Gregory Hanson and Ford Reeves cut a path through the vines and giant green tree leaves. They swung sharp machetes like hatchets or baseball bats.

Everyone walked in as straight a line as possible, stepping where the person ahead of them had stepped, mostly using a bent arm to push aside cut branches while ducking under the reach of hanging limbs.

Michael and Amber followed closely behind Reeves, Marshall was next, with Natalie, Tymere, and Hamilton behind him. Neeson, last in the slow moving line, was considered eerily important. Neeson ensured nothing dangerous stalked them.

It was only an hour into the jungle when the beautiful morning evaporated. Without any warning, it rained. They stopped and removed rain slickers from their packs. The slickers draped over their backpacks, as well.

There were only glimpses of the sky when looking up through the rainforest canopy. However, it had gotten somewhat darker each step they took into the dense foliage.

It wasn't a downpour, by any means. It rained steadily. The sound of the raindrops became almost soothing. The rain hit the leaves, the water ran off the leaves into a myriad of small streams, together, this drumming pattern sounded almost like music.

Under the cover of the leaves, and with the rain, the humidity decreased. Some. It actually felt a little cooler, but not cool. The heat, still apparent, dissipated enough so walking wasn't as laborious.

Footing became tricky. The already soft ground was muddier. Each step, the earth attempted sucking a foot deep into the saturated soil. The land they traversed, although mostly flat, did contain some hills.

They walked in mostly silence. The steady pace they kept, set by Hanson, chipped away at Michael's endurance.

As the hours passed, he found his breathing more labored. He wasn't tired, just not used to the constant exercise. Thankfully, his muscles weren't cramping up on him. Yet.

"Hey," Tymere called out. "Hold up."

Michael stopped walking and turned around. Tymere was on his knees. His hands dug into the mud. The others, who also stopped walking, moved around him. Hanson leaned against a tree.

Natalie, on her knees, watched closely as Tymere's excitement grew. He scooped away mud, only to have more slide into its place. Clearly, something burnt orange in color was below the surface.

"What is it?" Amber asked.

He carved around the edges of his find with his fingertips, and then pried from the dark mud a jagged piece of . . . something. "Ty?"

"It's a red clay pot. Natives would have dug clay out from the riverbanks. They would dig up mounds of clay and roll it into a rope," Tymere said, while still digging around the area where he found the small plate-sized shard. "They tie that rope into a knot, to test the endurance of the clay. They would have ground it up, added water to rehydrate the mix, throw in some sand, or, like, stone dust—to temper it. Next, they would shape it into a bowl, or like a frying pan. They would put, like, a rock into the concave part of the bowl, let it dry some, and then paddle the clay with something flat and hard, with the rock still inside. So the bowl didn't lose its shape. After letting it dry for a few weeks, they would carve designs on the outside, and then fire it."

Convinced the piece he found was the only artifact in this particular spot, he sat back on his heels and lifted the portion of a bowl toward his face for closer inspection. His eyes were open wide in awe, and he was smiling. "This is absolutely beautiful."

"Is it valuable?" Reeves asked.

Tymere shook his head. "Not really. I mean, if it were a complete thing—a bowl, or water jug or something, then maybe. But this? This is a piece of history."

Reeves looked as if he'd lost interest in the find.

Tymere handed the pottery to Natalie. "Put this in my backpack for me?" He turned around so she could push aside his slicker, unzip his pack, and insert it safely inside.

"There you go," she said. "Safe and sound."

"This is so awesome." Tymere reminded Michael of a child on Christmas morning. He couldn't help but savor the moment. "It is one thing spending time looking at pictures in books, telling me all about ancient pottery, where the author describes the color of the clay, and the texture, and the designs. But this is so much more than that. I mean, first of all, I found it. I actually dug it up from the earth. I'm getting to hold it in my hands and feel the texture, and see the red clay color with my own eyes. For me, this is absolutely unbelievable!"

"Pretty cool, Ty," Amber said. Tymere nodded, as if at a loss for words, his smile never fading.

"All right, then," Hanson said. "If we're good? We should be moving again."

9

Hanson stopped walking. He leaned against the base of a tree. Michael came up behind Hanson, and then stood beside him. His jaw nearly dropped to the wet, muddy ground. "Are you shitting me?"

Extending across a deep ravine, with jagged gunmetal grey rock formations below, were the remains of a crudely constructed swinging rope bridge. Knotted manila rope guide rails, as well as wooden planks for the base, extended in bowing fashion from one bank to the other.

"I've seen way too many movies," Michael said.

Amber squeezed between the two men. "Are you kidding me?"

"We have an issue?" Hanson asked.

"What's going on?" Natalie asked. Amber stepped aside. Natalie snaked her head through. "Um, I don't think so."

"No issue," Michael said. He focused on his girlfriend. "Honey, you can do this."

Hanson took a step away from the foot of the bridge so Tymere and Marshall could take a look at what swung out before them. "Here's the thing. This bridge is the only easy way across—"

"Easy?" Natalie questioned. "Have you ever crossed it before?"

"Not this bridge, specifically, no. But there are many bridges like this one out in the jungle. Hundreds. And there are people like us, my team and I, who make a living out in the rainforest. We realize it is in all of our best interests to ensure safe passage to and from the rivers," Hanson explained. "Although not the same bridge we've ever worked on, the work done is very similar. If you take notice, the rope there is relatively new. Probably not older than ten, maybe fifteen years."

Ten to fifteen year old rope did not sound comforting,

Michael thought. He replaced shoelaces every six months, or when he tried tying the laces one side was bound to snap free.

"The wooden planks there? It's Ipe. Seventy-five times harder than teak, and a hundred times better than any pressure-treated cedar or pine," Hanson said. "Whoever repaired this particular bridge was not concerned with pinching pennies."

Michael eyed the bridge. Repaired might be too loose a word. Yes, the planks looked solid. He didn't imagine anyone stepping on one and falling through. However . . . "How high up are we?" Michael asked.

Hanson held onto the post at the edge of the bridge and looked over the side. "I'd guess, at about the center of the bridge, it's two hundred to two-hundred-and-fifty feet down. My best guess."

"And across?"

"About the same across. Maybe three hundred feet?" Hanson scratched at his chin, eyeballing the opposite end of the bridge.

"And you guys put those planks in?" Tymere asked. He was at the foot of the bridge, kneeling closer to inspect the planks. He knocked on the wood, and looked back as if his knock confirmed the quality. "Looks solid."

"It is solid."

"You know what happens in the movies, right?" Marshall asked.

"In the movies the bridge is old, rickety. There are missing planks. And, if I am not mistaken, because we don't get to the theater too often out here in the jungle, there is usually a cannibalistic tribe chasing the main characters from one end, and impending doom awaiting the heroes on the other. Do I pretty much have it down?" Hanson cocked his head slightly to one side.

Michael did not appreciate the sarcasm. The man's true colors shined through clearer by the hour, it seemed. "And crocodiles," Michael said, unable to refrain.

"Excuse me?" Hanson asked.

Marshall understood. "In the raging river below, there were usually crocodiles."

"Crocodiles. Of course," Hanson said. "Well. This is how you can tell you are not part of some B-rated Hollywood production. Look down. You will not see any raging river. And I can promise you, there are zero crocodiles down there waiting to gnash your flesh and bones into ground beef."

Marshall looked over the edge of the bank and down the ravine. When he stood up straight and turned around, his face had become whiter. "It's like razor sharp rocks."

"See? No crocodiles," Hanson said. "Easy-peasy. Now, if you'll follow me."

Without delay, Hanson started across the bridge. He didn't even use the knotted rope rails to guide him on the way. He walked, sure footed and with purposeful strides, from one end toward the other. The bridge swayed in rhythm to his steps. However, it did look sturdy.

Easy-peasy. Michael gave Amber a shrug, and then gripped both rope rails in a hand. He held his foot over the first plank, as if dipping a toe into a knowingly cold swimming pool, and braced for the chill to race up his spine.

Michael knew Amber wasn't fond of heights. He recalled the one time they went on the Ferris wheel back in New York, at Darien Lake, in the sleepy town of Corfu. When it was built in 1982, it was considered the tallest Ferris wheel in the world. The giant wheel stood over one-hundred-and-sixty-five feet tall, and had forty stationary gondola carts for passengers. On the way up, she sat so close to him, but on the way down, she buried her head into his chest. And when the ride stopped with them at the very top, so riders could get off and on, she practically sat in his lap. It almost made him feel guilty for enjoying the ride while she was cursed with obvious discomfort, fear, and anxiety.

"Come on, we'll go across together. Won't seem too bad. Would have to be better than going across alone." Michael reached behind for her hand. She took it. He could feel how damp her skin was. It had nothing to do with the rain, nor the humidity. There was a difference.

"I wouldn't do that." Hamilton shook her head. "The rope is strong, the planks are solid. There's no doubt about that. Going two across, though? It's not something I'd recommend."

"You wouldn't?" Michael asked.

Hamilton eyed Amber. "I suppose the two of you can't weigh—"

"No," Amber halted the statement, squaring up her shoulders. "We don't need any more mishaps. You think only one at a time should cross. Then one at a time it is." She peered over the edge of the ravine. "Yeah. One at a time works."

"You want to go first?" Michael asked.

"I do." Amber thrust her arms straight down, hands curled into fists. "I mean, I don't, but I will. I'll go first, or next, after Gregory. Hanson."

"You sure?" Michael asked. "I'll be right behind you. Okay?"

Amber bit her lower lip. She nodded. Without another word, she walked onto the first plank. She held the rope guide rail in white knuckle grips. Only she had both hands on the same side of the bridge.

"Put your arms out like a T," Hamilton instructed. "One on either side of the bridge. You'll have better balance."

Amber shuffled from one plank to the next. She still only held onto one side of the rope. She moved her hands, one over the other, and then shuffled on to the next plank. It was slow going. Both Reeves and Neeson did not hide their frustrations. They took turns sighing out loud and rolling their eyes at one another.

Michael wanted Amber across before he addressed the issue with Hanson's team. At the moment, he was only concerned with Amber's advancement. "You got this," he said, encouragingly.

A quarter of the way across was when the bridge began to sway. The rain didn't help. When she moved her weight onto the next plank, her foot slipped. She dropped into a squat. She hooked her left arm under and around the rope guard rail. She did not appear to have been in danger of falling off the bridge. It would take a bit more than a tripped up step. The way she clutched the rope, and the way she had her eyes shut tight, Amber looked positive she'd come within an inch of losing her life. "Michael!"

Michael heard the terror in the cry for help.

It was pouring now. The rain came down in waves. It reminded Michael of the overhead sprays in a carwash. A mist rose from below and rolled, as if a river, along the bottom of the ravine.

Michael tried not to imagine crocodiles suddenly appearing from the bowels of the mist. "Get up, Amber. You can do this."

"We really don't have all day," Neeson said. It was a hushed comment. Perhaps only Hamilton and Reeves were meant to hear it.

Michael spun around on them. "She's scared, all right? She's scared. Crossing a bridge like this, out here, isn't something she's used to, okay? But let me tell you what she is used to doing, and that's saving lives. Every day she rides in the back of an ambulance, treating heart attacks, gunshot wounds, and taking care of people beaten with crowbars, stabbed with screwdrivers, or after having been gang raped in the parking lot behind some club. When Marshall wasn't breathing, it was Ty who jumped in and pulled him out, and Amber who brought him back to life. So you know what? A little more respect, huh? She's earned that. She definitely deserves at least that much from all of you. From all of us."

Michael walked out onto the bridge.

Hamilton reached for his arm. "I would advise against two people on the bridge at once," she said.

He shrugged free of her grasp. "I'm willing to risk it."

Once on the bridge, he felt his muscles tense. A little panic rose inside him. With his arms out in a T, he took hold of the rope guide rail and ambled forward. When he reached Amber, she had her head down. She was crying.

He put his hands on her shoulders. He let his legs work to keep his balance as the bridge swayed back and forth. It hadn't looked that bad from the one bank. Out here on the bridge, however, it was a completely different story. It made him remember standing on a swing at the park when he was a child. Sitting and swinging had been too easy for any five year old. Instead, he recalled standing on the seat, holding the chains, and swinging as high as he could. The fear didn't set in until, on one particular swing, slack caught in the chain, and the motion of swinging became jerky instead of smooth and consistent.

That was how he felt now. As if there was suddenly slack in the ropes, and the bridge was jerking back and forth. He wondered if it was in his mind, but Michael thought the wind had picked up and there was a whistling sound to its movement. Were the planks creaking? Did it sound as if the rope was weakening under the strain of his weight? The noises, real or imagined, filled his head. On top of that, he could hear his own breathing and his heart beating.

Michael knelt beside her. He put his lips near her ear. "You remember our second date?"

"Not now," she said. He saw her eyes were shut tight.

"Our second date we went to Six Flags, remember?"

"The Ferris wheel," she said.

"Right. The Ferris wheel."

"I only went on it because I knew you wanted to."

"When you got scared, you sat close to me."

"You held me the whole time."

"I did." He slowly stood up, his hand leading hers. "And you made it until the end of the ride."

"I felt safe with you," she said.

"We can do this. Together," he said. "Stand up with me, Amber."

He helped her back up onto her feet. She tried facing one way, and holding the same side of the guide rail with both hands. Without words he turned her so she faced the opposite end of the bridge, and so they both held a side of the rope guide rail in each hand.

Michael broke the cardinal rule whenever one is too high off the ground. Never look down. He only peered over fleetingly, but it was enough. Aside from swift moving mist, he saw clearly the jutting rock formations, like stalagmites at the bottom of a cave. Additionally, there were tree tops, and fallen trees where the break at the trunks was far from a clean snap. Instead, the tree trunks reminded Michael of a mound of stakes one might use to drive through the heart of a vampire.

Falling from the bridge meant certain death. There was no way to survive such a fall. The distance from the bridge to the ground alone would kill a man. The rocks and the tree limbs, and stakes, however, would ensure a most painful and gruesome death, to boot.

Michael shivered. He closed his eyes and lifted his head. When he once again opened his eyes, he was looking dead ahead. All that mattered at that point was crossing to the other side. Forget what he had seen below them. Forget it and move past it, move across it.

Move over it.

"One foot after the other," he whispered. He said it calmly, softly. It was meant to reassure both of them. Once Amber started walking again, he knew it had worked. "That's it. One foot after the other."

The wooden planks were close together. There was little gap between each plank. It wasn't like they had to jump from one to the other. And it wasn't as if they could fall between planks. The overall construction of the bridge was quite impressive.

Halfway across was the worst. The motion from swaying was at the climax at this point. Michael kept closing his eyes against nauseousness. "We got this," he whispered close to her ear.

"We got this," she agreed. "We got this."

They both said those words over and over as they continued forward until, eventually, they made it to the other side.

Hanson put a hand on Amber's shoulder. "Well done. Sit and have some water. You've earned it."

Michael sat with Amber and sipped from her canteen as they watched the others cross the bridge rather effortlessly.

Neeson walked over. Michael was ready for another confrontation. Instead, Neeson took a knee in front of Amber. "Hey. You did really good out there. Really good. You might have been afraid of heights before, but no one can take crossing a bridge like that away from you."

He put out a fist. She gently smashed knuckles with her own fist. "Thank you," she said, her lower lip trembling. Her shoulders shook.

Hamilton came over next. "Nice job, Amber."

"Thank you," she said.

Reeves approached and gave her two thumbs up.

She returned the gesture, and then looked at Michael. "Wasn't that nice of them?"

"Very," he said.

"Albright!" Hanson called out.

"Be right back," Michael said. He went over to Hanson, who still stood by the end of the rope bridge. "Yeah?"

"Something happen on the other side with members of my team?"

Michael looked back at Amber. Hamilton and Neeson sat on

either side of Amber. It looked as if they were both telling her some elaborate story. He heard Amber laughing, and Neeson nodding, as if guilty of some ridiculous encounter that must have left him looking less than macho.

"Nah," Michael said. "Everything's good."

10

Finding a place to camp for the night felt random. It was an open spot with tall trees spaced out enough for them to string a grey tarp roof between them, and another on the ground, and then hung off-white netting from the top tarp down to the ground covering tarp. Everyone pitched in setting up the makeshift tent. It felt good getting out of the steady rain. There was no chance they would dry, though. Shrugging off the rain slicker, Michael sighed with some relief.

Hanson announced they'd covered sixteen miles. While Michael was impressed, Hanson did not appear happy with the progress.

Neeson removed thin rectangular what looked like dirt-brown potato chip bags from his pack. He tossed one to each of the eight of them, keeping one for himself. "Dinner is served. *Bon appetit.*"

Amber wrinkled her nose, looking the bag over. "Dinner?"

"They're M-R-Es," Tymere volunteered.

"Meals Ready to Eat," Hamilton added.

"Beef stroganoff and cobbler pie?" Amber said.

"Mine is meatballs and marinara sauce with a brownie," Natalie said.

Hanson opened his pouch, removed the independently wrapped dessert, and then added water to the bag. "Trust me. Not as bad as they look. They taste pretty good, actually." He held the bag closed and shook it. "Also, quite filling. About twelve hundred calories in each package."

Michael and Amber locked eyes. He wished they'd encountered some fruit along the way. Berries. Anything. They hadn't. Instead of complaining, he furrowed his brow and did his best to smile. "Well. Let's dig in."

In truth the food wasn't bad, Michael admitted as he finished his meal. "The chocolate chip cookie was soft, and moist."

"Right?" Reeves said. "Not too shabby."

It began raining a little harder. Michael looked up at the tarp. It sounded like a demonic drum solo. Beyond the LED lanterns lighting the inside of the tent was complete darkness.

The sounds in the jungle were different at night than during the day. Michael couldn't hear birds singing, or monkeys chit-chatting. Yes, there was an occasional bird, still awake, letting out a chirp here and there, and what could be a monkey saying something to another.

Instead, the beyond seemed more infinite, and ominous.

Over the steady din of the rain, insects gave a concert. Something sounded like it was whistling every few seconds. Something hammered into a nearby tree, the sound not unlike one a woodpecker made.

The sounds, in and of themselves, were not unsettling as much as the black that surrounded them. The black almost had weight. Was it pressing down on them? Closing in on them. The black generated an almost claustrophobic sensation.

They sat around one of the bright LED lanterns. Ford Reeves stood outside of the netting, smoking a cigar. The odor from the smoke reminded Michael of his grandfather. When he was a boy and visited with his parents, Michael always remembered seeing his grandfather sitting outside in the garage. He had green indoor-outdoor carpeting on the cement floor. It was plush, almost as if grass. There were always extra aluminum folding chairs. The one next to his grandfather was always reserved for Michael. He considered it the biggest honor, too. They both did. Michael and his father would sit and talk with his grandfather, but Michael's mother would always wrinkle her nose at the smell of cigar smoke and go into the house to visit with her mother-in-law. At such a young age, Michael had no idea the ill effects brought on by tobacco. All he knew was he adored the aroma. He would watch his grandfather take a puff, hold the smoke in his mouth a moment, and then blow perfect rings. The scent of a bouquet of floral notes, and something sweet, like cherries.

Reeves must have been smoking a similar brand of cigar, because the memories flooded Michael's mind.

Marshall had his phone out. He texted, but before putting his phone away, he smiled at the screen.

"Ah," Natalie said. "What was that?"

Marshall looked suddenly guilty, raising his eyebrows and looking around too innocently. "What was what?"

"Your text. I actually saw you texting on the boat, as well," Natalie said. "Which isn't a big deal, other than that grin you're wearing."

"It isn't the grin, so much as the blushing," Tymere added.

Marshall touched his cheeks. "I'm not blushing. It's the lighting. The light only makes it look like I'm blushing."

Amber laughed. "Oh my goodness. Who is she?"

Michael noticed the sheepish look exchanged between Neeson and Hamilton. Michael also noted Hanson catching the same trade. If the two members of his team thought they were pulling a fast one on the boss, they were clearly mistaken.

"Marshall," Natalie prodded.

"Fine. I—well—I did meet a young lady a few weeks ago. I planned on telling everyone. It's just, I figured before I said anything, I would wait and see if it was really going anywhere," Marshall admitted.

Michael said, "Well, who is she? Do we know her?"

"Is she someone from school?" Tymere asked.

"She's not from school," Marshall said. He dropped eye contact with everyone. "You—ah, you know her, Mikey."

Michael pointed at himself. "I do? But no one else?"

"I suspect Amber might know her as well," Marshall said.

"Me?" Amber asked.

"You're killing us with the suspense, Marshall. Killing us," Natalie proclaimed. She had her hands balled into fists and shook them, as if in agony.

"Well," Marshall started, "she's your cousin, Mikey. Annabelle."

"Annabelle?" Michael sounded miffed. He sat up straighter. "How on earth would you have met . . ."

Amber seemed to have caught on as well.

"My father's funeral?" Michael asked.

"I mean, I wasn't expecting to meet someone at a funeral. You have to believe me. We were outside, talking by the hors d'oeuvres . One thing kind of led to another." Marshall held up both hands, as if surrendering. "But if you don't want me talking with your cousin, I'll end it."

Michael let Marshall stew in his own discomfort for a moment. "You two really like each other?"

Marshall grinned again. Michael saw the blushing rosy-up his friend's cheeks. "We do."

"She is lucky to have met a guy like you," Michael said. Amber took his hand in her own.

"You mean that?" Marshall sounded surprised. His voice went up half an octave. It was almost as if he were entering puberty, and his tone cracked.

"Of course I mean that. You're both lucky. Annabelle's one of my favorite cousins."

"She said you were her favorite cousin, as well," Marshall said.

"As long as we're all confessing things . . ." Natalie said.

"We are?" Amber laughed.

Natalie took hold of her necklace, unveiling a ring that had been tucked down the front of her shirt.

Amber got to her feet, and moved closer. "Is that . . . is that what I think it is? You guys are engaged?"

Michael watched Tymere's expression tighten. His mouth closed so that his lips almost sucked up into nothing.

"Well," Natalie said. "It's a promise ring."

"What's a promise ring?" Neeson asked. He looked bewildered, brow furrowed.

Natalie rocked her head from side to side. "It is a ring promising that we will get engaged."

Neeson didn't even try to mask his laugh. "What does that mean? Isn't that what an engagement ring is? A promise to get married? This is where he promises he will get engaged, which is a promise to get married? It's a third step?"

Hanson waved a hand. "Chuck! That's enough."

Tymere defended the ring. "That's exactly what it is. We've only been together a little over a year and a half. We have to finish college still—"

"Why not call it an engagement ring?" Neeson asked. He shook his head. "Only in America."

Hamilton grimaced. "You're from Detroit."

"That's not the point," he answered.

"That's enough," Hanson said, more forcefully this time. "Look, I suggest we turn in and try and get a good night's sleep.

Believe it or not, morning will come fast. Tomorrow, we're going to pick up the pace. We have a lot of ground to cover to reach your target area in two days."

Neeson held out a hand. "Look, I didn't mean anything by that. I had never heard of a promise ring before. No hard feelings?"

Tymere shook his hand. "No. None."

"Natalie, I would like to wish you both sincere congratulations."

"Thank you," she said.

Next, Amber, Marshall, and Michael congratulated Tymere and Natalie.

"You guys *just* did this, didn't you?" Michael asked.

"When we were at the hotel in Brazil," Natalie said. She still smiled. She still looked happy, and excited. Her eyes showed her true emotions.

Michael knew this had to be why they had been so extra lovey-dovey on the helicopter. They had their romantic secret. It gave them a power, a peace, over the fear of the flight itself.

"I'm really happy for you guys. I am," he said.

"Thank you, Mikey," they each said, and hugged him.

Once they were all settled in for bed, the jungle became even more alive. Frogs croaked and an array of animals Michael did not recognize at all squeaked and squealed. There were hoots, and squelching barks. There was a definite pattern to it all. A cacophony, a chorus, of music that blended perfectly.

If it weren't so loud, it would have been almost calming.

"You okay?" Amber whispered.

"It's so loud."

"What do you think about the promise ring?" she asked.

It was too late for this kind of conversation. He saw the traps laid out, as well. He did not want to fall victim to any of them. "We can talk about it tomorrow."

"You going to be able to fall asleep?" she asked.

At least sleeping on the tarp was soft. Maybe a bit too mushy, but it beat settling down on a bed of rocks.

"Hugging you this close and tight? Without any problem," he assured her.

With that, she snuggled in closer, pulled his arm over her neck, and tucked his hand under the side of her cheek. It was far from comfortable for him, but he knew sleeping like this made her feel safe and secure.

Michael heard Tymere and Natalie whispering. He hoped Neeson's remarks hadn't spoilt their moment. He couldn't hear what they said. The sleeping arrangements were far from ideal. The nine of them packed together under a tarp was a little too close for comfort. Hanson and his team laid down and seemed to fall immediately to sleep. He wondered if it was a military thing, like there was a way they trained their bodies to respond and react, on command.

Before long, Michael let the songs of the jungle soothe him. The rain let up some, and he found he could barely keep his eyes open any longer. He wasn't sure why he was fighting sleep in the first place.

Hanson was brutally honest with them. Michael did not doubt they would double-time their hike efforts. He hoped his legs and feet weren't an aching mess come morning.

11

The morning did come fast. Hanson made it clear there was little time to dilly-dally, as he had put it. They went in pairs into the jungle to take care of morning bathroom rituals, then ate breakfast, folded up camp, and got back into the heat of hiking.

Michael had been one hundred percent correct about Hanson. He'd cut a path through the vines and leaves with fervor. The swatches he slashed through the terrain were both clean, and wide. The trail being created should be easy to identify when it was time to return to the boat.

Hanson stopped at one point and knelt by fallen trees. The bark was covered in thick, green moss. Sprouting from the moss were mushrooms. "The humidity and heat make the perfect breeding ground for mushrooms," Hanson said. "There are countless varieties growing in this jungle. What you have to be careful of is knowing the difference between which ones you can eat, and which ones to avoid."

The others had caught up, and everyone stood gathered around Hanson as he gave them a lesson in fungi. Above was a break in the forest canopy and the blue sky was hampered by a sheer grey, gauze-like cloud. Michael was thankful it was not, yet, raining. He still didn't feel dry from the previous day. He thought his skin might still be wrinkling beneath his clothing.

"Is there a way to tell what mushrooms are consumable?" Marshall knelt beside Hanson and picked a mushroom stem from the moss. He held the fungi closer to his face for better inspection. The stem was off-white, thick, and long. The cap better resembled an inverted pyramid. What looked like veins on a leaf were visible on the exposed mushroom cap underside. The patch of mushrooms looked more like unmoving sea anemones than fungi. He smelled the rim of the mushroom and shrugged. "Doesn't really smell like anything."

"Takes an expert, I suppose. What I do know is that these

are Yanomami mushrooms, and they are safe to eat. They sell them in marketplaces around Brazil. They are very distinct looking." Hanson plucked a mushroom from the moss, as well. "The thing about mushrooms is simple. There are three possible outcomes from eating one if you know nothing about the fungi. One, you eat it and it is delicious, and nothing happens. Or, two, you eat it, and for the next five hours you are high as a kite and tripping—"

"There are psychedelic mushrooms growing in here?" Tymere asked; he also knelt and picked a mushroom from the moss for closer inspection. His fingertip traced the veins from the stem up the inverted cap, as if he'd discovered an alien lifeform.

"Absolutely, just like the ones that grow up in Alaska, but more potent, I suspect," Hanson said. "So there is that. And then there is number three. This is perhaps the more common effect. You get deathly ill, and, or, die. So picking and eating random mushrooms gives you a one-in-three chance you won't entirely mess up your day. So, these being mushrooms that I know for a fact are safe to eat, I say we collect a few for dinner tonight. Adds a little something extra to the MREs, don't you think?"

Chuck Neeson shook open a small, brown paper bag. Michael and his friend plucked mushrooms and dropped them into the bag until Hanson indicated it was time to get moving once again.

They covered a lot of ground. The fact it was not raining helped. However, the ground they stepped on was less forgiving. Everything was wet and slippery. There was either mud everywhere, or small streams, as if a few of the tall trees had sprung leaks. The musty air was thick and damp. Michael thought he could feel it enter his lungs with each breath he took.

The biggest hindrance was the bugs. The flying insects. They were everywhere. Waving a hand through a scourge of mosquitoes was fruitless. The repellent they sprayed on their clothing carried minimal impact at diverting the bugs from attempting to penetrate exposed skin and feast on sweet human blood. Malaria and Yellow Fever were very common illnesses caused by mosquito bites in Brazil. Both diseases were seriously dangerous. Two-hundred-and-ninety-million people are diagnosed with malaria each year; of those infected, nearly four-hundred-thousand will die. Chills and a high fever are a clear sign someone has contracted the disease. Headaches, nausea, and jaundice, a yellowing of the skin and the whites of the eyes, are an indication of Yellow Fever. Michael did not want any of them to encounter either of these diseases, which was why he had insisted they all receive vaccinations against Typhoid, Hepatitis A, and Yellow Fever prior to their leaving of the States.

"Maybe we can have a big smoky fire tonight?" Amber asked. She waved her hand in front of her face like a fan. She wrinkled her nose, squinted her eyes, and blew air from pursed lips, trying to keep the mosquitoes off any part of her head.

"It will be difficult finding wood and kindling dry enough to start a fire, but I agree," Hamilton said. "We should give it a try—Stop, Michael!"

Without a question, Michael stopped. He didn't duck, he didn't step back. He just stopped. That was the command, and he followed it.

Hamilton approached him from behind. He could hear her boots crunch on sticks, getting sucked at by the mud.

The entire parade stopped. No one was moving. No one except Angelina Hamilton. Michael realized he was holding his breath. His lungs began burning, but he was afraid to even let out air. His mouth went dry. He had no idea what kind of danger he was in.

"Don't move a muscle." Hamilton was close. Her voice came across in a whisper. It was as if she had her lips beside his ear and no one else around could hear her instruction.

"Oh my God," Amber said. "Don't move, Michael."

"I'm not," he said, between clenched teeth. He knew he was sweating profusely now. The sweat had nothing at all to do with the heat or humidity. The beaded balls of perspiration were birthed from the growing creases along his brow, and rolled down his forehead and into his eyes. He ignored the salty sting as best he could. "What is it?"

"A spider," Amber whispered.

"A Brazilian Wandering Spider," Ford Reeves said. "Badass arachnids, that's for sure."

"Yeah, I figured as much," Michael managed, "when

Hamilton told me not to move a muscle."

"Good thinking, Angelina," Reeves added.

"How, ah, how big?" Michael asked.

Reeves moved around so he could stand in front of Michael. "It's like six inches with the legs. The body," he shrugged, "eh, it's only like two inches."

"They're poisonous, right?" Michael asked.

"Actually, no," Marshall said. "They're venomous."

"Same thing!" Michael said, teeth clenched.

"It's not. Venomous is defined as when something bites, or stings you, and the venom is then . . . injected," Marshall explained. "Whereas poisonous would be—"

"Stop. Stop. Stop," Michael said. "I don't care."

"Well. He's not wrong," Reeves added.

Michael knew his heart was pounding. "Okay, okay. So why aren't we doing anything? Why isn't someone swatting this thing off me?"

Hamilton said, "You see, it's perched right at your collar. It must have scurried up your leg when you were all picking mushrooms. Unless provoked, they won't bite."

"It's right by your neck, Mikey," Tymere said. "Like, the back legs are on your collar, and the fangs are so close to your skin."

"It's covered in hair, like a tarantula," Natalie said.

"I so, so, did not need to know that, Nat," Michael said. If someone didn't do something soon, he thought he might faint. He knew his legs were close to giving out. He could feel the adrenaline coursing through him, but the secreting hormone did not aid his courage. Fight, flight . . . or faint. Those seemed like the only options available.

"A bite from this spider is said to be super painful." Michael wished Reeves would stop talking. "The good news is, in nineteen-ninety-six, I think, an antidote was found, or created. You know what I mean?"

"Well, that's good. That's very good," Michael said. He finally felt relieved. He preferred not to get bitten at all. At least if he were bitten, he wasn't going to die. "Do you guys have some? Do you have, like, an antidote shot in one of your bags?"

"We don't," Hanson said flatly. He stood behind Reeves, arms crossed. He wore a stone-faced expression. It was completely void of any concern or emotion.

Amber said, "If this spider bites him—"

Hamilton shook her head. "We don't want this spider to bite him. You saw how much ground we've covered in the last several days. It could be three or four days before we get him to a hospital."

"Maybe longer," Reeves said, "because at least two of you would have to be carrying him back through the jungle. That's going to slow everything down."

"So what are we doing?" Marshall said. "How long are we going to stay here and talk about this before someone just—"

Amber moved fast. She stepped forward and smacked the spider off Michael's back with a sweep of her hand. After, she pulled her arm back in and hugged it to her chest, her hand folded in on itself. She danced in place. "There. All done. No more problems!"

"You got it?" Michael asked.

"She got it," Hamilton confirmed.

"Well, holy shit," Reeves said. "That was messed up, right there, but I like it. That spider just as easily could have bitten your hand. Then they'd be carrying you back through the forest, trying to make it to a hospital before you died."

Amber tried masking her fear. It wasn't working. There was a slight quiver in her lower lip. "Something had to be done. You were all going to stand around and do nothing—"

"I was waiting for it to relax," Hamilton said. "That spider was as aware of all of us as we were of it. It was agitated. The spider was ready to bite as a defense to us all staring at it. Once it calmed down, and moved off of Michael's collar, I would have knocked it away. It would have been less dangerous for him, and for me."

"I did not realize that," Amber admitted.

"Either way, the threat has been eliminated, and we still have miles to go."

Michael brushed at his shoulders, and did a bit of a dance on his tippy toes. Then he quickly ran his fingers through his hair and shook his head.

"It's gone, dude," Tymere said.

Michael swept his hands down the thighs of his pants. "I feel like there are a ton of those things still on me."

"You didn't even get to see what it looked like," Tymere said.

"It wasn't that bad?" Michael asked.

Tymere shook his head. "Oh, no. It was bad. Bigger than I expected. Covered in hair. I saw like eight million eyes, and fangs like Dracula!"

Natalie gave Tymere a playful shove. "Stop teasing!"

"There's none on you, honey," Amber said. "It's all gone."

Michael gave Amber a kiss, then he spun around. "All gone? There's none on me?"

"No. None." Amber turned around. "But to be safe, how about on me?"

Tymere, Natalie, and Marshall all spun around, as well. They took turns checking each other for spiders. No one else had one on them. They were clear. That didn't mean more spiders weren't on the ground all around them.

Michael found it difficult walking without staring at his feet. Little by little, he became fully aware he felt more afraid. By the hour. By the minute. How had his father spent a lifetime lost in isolated jungles, crossing the wastelands of Antarctica, and diving into shark infested waters? Had the man been crazy, or fearless?

It must have been an insane mixture of the two. Michael began to think he wasn't cut out in any way, shape, or form to follow in his father's footsteps. The realization that this entire venture was a mistake sank in, and it hurt his heart. One dangerous mishap after another only accented the truth.

What in the world had he gotten them into? Hopefully the worst of it all was now behind them. He couldn't imagine things ever getting much worse. Otherwise, how would they get out of this alive?

12

Less Than a Day Behind Albright

Nicholas Katic followed closely behind Rosemary as they traipsed through the overgrowth of the jungle. His two guides stayed in front of them, carving a path. Nicholas suspected they kept on the same route as Albright and his team, since a lot of the growth looked as if it was already cut away.

"How are you doing, Father?" Rosemary asked, without turning around. She held an unused machete in one hand and, with the other, she waved away the insistent mosquitoes that flew around in front of her face. Every now and then she snorted through her nostrils, launching free the insects finding refuge inside her nose.

"I'm good," he said. He wasn't sure his response was the *complete* truth. The years spent in a cushy curator position had done his body no favors. How fast his muscle had given way to mush. The burn had started in his thighs yesterday. Before long, his back was achy, and his feet felt swollen inside his boots. He worried if he took them off at night, he would not be able to put them back on in the morning.

Nicholas knew it was his heavy breathing that prompted Rosemary's inquiry. He found himself focusing intently on each breath. Thankfully, the trek had been across mostly flat ground. If they had to hike up ridges, hills, and mountains, he might not be faring half as well as he was.

The monkeys in the trees were very active. They hooted and hollered with enthusiasm. Perhaps they chatted about Nicholas and his group as they crossed over leaves, twigs, and branches below? Birds sang loud, long songs. Others simply let out annoyed squeaks and tweets, while some cawed.

Nicholas, used to the endless jabbering sounds of the jungle, noticed Rosemary continually glance up toward the Amazon canopy. The funny thing about the forest was that regardless of all the sound, whether it was fluttering, or the snapping of branches, most of the animals remained hidden. Once in a while he caught sight of wings flapping, or something jumping from one tree to another. Usually, though, there was nothing to be seen.

"I'm out of shape," he added. *Terribly out of shape*, he thought.

"I know. I can hear you breathing. Do you want to take a break? We can stop for a bit. Take a minute for you to rest," she offered. She never stopped trudging forward, and neither did he. They kept pressing on.

"I'll be fine. It's getting late, and we'll be stopping soon for the night, anyway," he said.

"You're sure?"

He wasn't.

"I am," he said.

It never should have come to this. The pirate's buried treasure should have been discovered decades ago. This was Alexander's fault. He was there the day the jaguars attacked, and yes, it had been unfortunate. However, that should never have been a cause to end the expeditions.

Nicholas knew Alexander had an office full of research. Each book, document, map led toward answers, toward some undiscovered tomb, crypt, priceless find. The infuriating man hoarded away information, all of the evidence needed for discovery. Selfishly, Alexander deprived the world of the excitement deserved at uncovering ancient treasures!

Nicholas had nothing against Michael and his friends. They were getting in over their heads. Their combined backgrounds amounted to nothing when it came to treasure hunting. This trip was little more than a whim for them, a summer fling. If he allowed them to find Roche Braziliano's buried treasure, they wouldn't know what to do with it. They would make some crazy announcement, and maybe sell off the find to the highest bidder.

Treasure hunting might be about making some money, but it was also about preservation. He was certain his own museum would purchase Brazilliano's treasure, but the amount wouldn't make Michael and his friends millionaires.

Michael was already well off. Nicholas was certain of it. Alexander died a rich man. With no other kin, he had no doubt

Michael inherited every last penny.

Not to mention, Michael also had access to all of Alexander's extensive research.

He tried forming a friendship, an alliance, where the two of them could work together completing Alexander's work, but no, Michael wanted nothing to do with such a generous offer.

Despite, or in spite, of all of the aforementioned, it had little to do with this particular trip. Rosemary was indeed the true focus behind the mission. Nicholas refused to lose sight of the validity, the required —*essential*— validation!

Now, here they all were, being eaten alive by mosquitoes, trudging through the Amazon in the middle of summer. He was far too old to be out here doing this, far too out of shape. This is what Michael's own selfishness reduced him to. Like father like son, he supposed.

His foot sank in the mud. The mud gripped the sole of his boot. He planted his walking stick firmly in front of him. He leaned his weight forward and lifted his boot out of the mud. It made a sickening sucking sound. It reminded him of mud pies he made as a kid. With a spoon from the kitchen drawer, and a pitcher of water from the refrigerator, he'd sit in the backyard at first digging a hole deep into the earth, and then, finally, mixing in the water. He would slap it together with his hands and make the mound into pie shapes. It was all fun and good until his mother came around to check on him, and would then freak out over her ruined, bent silverware.

He scraped the excess mud off on a nearby fallen moss-covered tree limb.

"Father?"

"I'm right behind you," he said dismissively and waved a hand in the air. He didn't need Rosemary worrying needlessly. He could tell something was occupying her mind. He assumed she struggled with the end game, and was having second thoughts. And yet, here they were. Together. Pressing on. He would not give up. He had no intention of giving in. Life was about moving forward, always getting ahead. Tired, old, out of shape, or not, it was about *always* moving forward. "I'm okay."

It was hard not remembering the day the jaguars attacked. In fact, the images haunted many of his dreams, and made getting a full night's sleep near impossible at times. There were probably close to twenty thousand jaguars in the jungle. Maybe more.

With nearly 200,000 acres burned down each day, 78 million acres a year, the deforestation had forced animals out, shrinking their natural habitat footprint. They were packed in tighter and tighter, making the rainforest overcrowded in terms of predator territory. Running into a jaguar this time around was probably even *more* likely now than it had been twenty-some years ago, while on expedition with Alexander.

As he caught up with Rosemary, Nicholas scanned the forest canopy, just as Rosemary had been doing. Only he wasn't looking for monkeys or exotic birds.

The thing with jaguars, Nicholas knew, if he actually saw one . . . it was already too late.

13

Chuck Neeson started a fire. It was no small feat. He searched for wood dry enough to burn for nearly an hour, while the others set up camp for the night.

Michael put in extra effort ensuring no spiders had found their way onto the tarp after the netting was secured in place. He checked every inch of the tarp more than once. Far from satisfied, he sat by his gear, but his eyes scanned the tarp for unnatural movement.

"You okay?" Amber asked.

"Still a bit freaked out," he said. The funny thing was, he never saw the spider. It had been on his back, and was knocked away. Once it hit the ground, it must have scurried under the foliage. That didn't matter. He had phantom symptoms, and continually brushed at his shoulder.

The smoke from the fire served a purpose. The bugs seemed annoyed and, for the most part, stayed away from camp, despite the LED lights from the battery-operated lanterns. He hoped the smoke kept spiders away, as well.

Hanson poured the berries and mushrooms they'd collected throughout the day into separate piles. "We made some real good time today. Covered a lot of ground. My Garmin indicates by *noonish* tomorrow, we should be within the area you designated."

Michael's legs and feet felt as if they'd hiked over twenty miles, just today. Relatively speaking, they weren't all that far inland. At this pace, it would take a month to reach the center of the Amazon. He supposed the ancient pirate figured three to four days into the jungle was plenty when it came to hiding his treasure. He would have been correct, too. It wasn't as if they could drive a Jeep through this part of the rainforest, although such a luxury would have been nice.

Tymere and Marshall stood up, Ty with a roll of toilet paper and a small, collapsible shovel. "This is probably the worst part of the trip," he groaned. "Makes me feel less than . . . civilized."

They parted the netting, and waved their way past the smoky campfire.

"Bury it deep," Reeves called after them. "We don't need animals sniffing around, and we sure don't want to get any whiffs, either!"

"Crude," Amber whispered.

"Mr. Albright," Hanson said. "I was wondering if I could take a look at the map you carry, for verification. I want to be sure we are, indeed, headed to the right longitude and latitude you provided prior to the excursion."

Michael found the request peculiar. The coordinates would not have changed. At no time had Michael ever shown Hanson the actual map. Part of the reason, he wanted to keep the exact location his father marked private. The spot wasn't guaranteed. The placement was based on his father's own research, reviewing of historical documents, and parts of the pirate's recovered journal.

The other reason made less sense. He worried Hanson and his team might steal the map. A simple, and plausible concept, that really carried little weight. Once they reached the area tomorrow afternoon, after they retrieved any found treasure, what stopped the guides from *then* taking what they wanted?

Hanson and his guide members had the weapons. The real weapons.

Hanson had never before asked to see the actual map. His asking to review it now actually made sense. It made more sense than Michael's reasons not to share the map. However, he felt uncomfortable. Now put on the spot, if Michael declined the request, it made him look suspect. It would pique the curiosity of the others on Hanson's team.

A guide had been essential for the success of the journey, Michael knew. Only now he wished they had gone this route alone. Which, of course, was not something they could have accomplished.

Hanson held out his hand.

Michael caught Amber's eye. Her expression looked as if it matched his own thoughts. Her lips were pressed closed, and her eyebrows were both a bit arched. How could he deny

Hanson, though?

He couldn't.

He reached into his vest pocket. The map was folded inside a waterproof Ziplock bag. He pulled open the bag and removed the map. Without unfolding it, he held out the map.

Both Michael and Hanson kept a hand on a corner of the folded document for a long moment. Their eyes met. In that instant, Michael knew his personal conflict was realized. He released the map.

Hanson held it out between them and smiled.

"Let me set your mind at ease, sir. This, guiding people, is our livelihood, okay? If we screw over our customers, how long do you think we could stay in business?" Hanson unfolded the map, slowly. His eyes never left Michael's eyes.

Michael looked away first. Hanson's team were all staring at him, mouths dropped. Although he had said nothing, Hanson's insinuation was enough. He'd insulted every one of them.

"I said nothing of the kind." Michael's defensive stance sounded weak and shallow. He didn't buy it any more than Hanson's team bought it.

"Sure, it is," Hanson said. He held the map open, then set it down on a makeshift table. He lifted an LED lantern and set it on a corner of the map. "Well, holy cow. Will you take a look at this?"

Hamilton, Reeves, and Neeson crowded around their boss.

"Roche Braziliano?" Reeves asked.

"Old pirate," Hanson said. "He wasn't much of a terror back in the sixteen-fifties? Sixties? But he did roam eastern parts of Brazil back then. Supposedly. At some point he went where all pirates migrated, the Caribbean. However, it seems the mate was a bit of an explorer, as well. Do I have that correct, Albright?"

Michael knew it was now all or nothing. There was no changing the turn of events. The guides, clearly enthralled, wanted more explanation, revelation. He couldn't clam-up and leave them with nothing. He wasn't positive how or why he knew this much, but felt if he left them hanging, Hanson would find a way to draw the rest of the information out of him.

"There wasn't too much written about the pirate, however, the man did a bit of writing on his own. My father—"

"That would be Doctor Alexander Albright," Hanson added.

Michael knew he'd found Gregory Hanson's name written among his father's possessions. Thinking back on it now, he remembered there had been a line through the name and phone number. At the time, Michael had assumed, for one reason or another, Hanson wasn't able to partake on a specific expedition, and so his father had crossed him off a list of possible guides. Now, Michael wondered if, when his father crossed out Hanson's name, it had been for a completely different reason.

"That's correct."

"I knew your father. Did some work with him, back when I was fresh out of the military and getting this venture off the ground. It was, like, twenty years ago, back before he retired from treasure hunting." Hanson was standing up straight while his team studied the map. "Is that what you guys are doing? Picking up where the old man left off? Going after buried treasure?"

"I suppose," Michael admitted. In for a penny, in for a pound. "We aren't really expecting to find anything. Not really. This fall, we go into our senior year of college and we wanted something monumental, some big adventure to remember. Because after graduation, you know—" Almost flippant, Hanson waved a hand. "Oh, I know. Real life. No more dorms and cafeteria food, or all-nighters studying for exams. Instead, it becomes about paying the bills. Student loans must be bigger than a house mortgage these days. Life steps in. You're worried after graduation, that's it. Your friendships will suffer."

Neeson turned around. "It will. It happens all the time." He moved away from the map. He sat on his bedding, feet down, knees up. He wrapped his arms around his legs. "You do the old, 'Hey, let's keep in touch.'" He changed the sound of his voice for the statement, "Ya never do."

"Sure, you do," Hamilton added. She also moved away from the map and went over to where she would be sleeping. "At first, anyway. You get together for lunch, or drinks, every couple of weeks. Then it is every couple of months. After a year, it becomes so sporadic. Someone can't make it that day, so you propose another. Someone else can't make that new date, so you all agree to try again the following month."

"Hate that," Neeson said. "Because it doesn't work. Too many other things fill the free time until you have, like, zero free time. There's a husband, or a wife. Like with you and your boyfriend. After that actual wedding ring replaces the promise ring, the two of you have family things going on. Probably kids, and jobs, and bills."

Natalie pursed her lips. "We'll have those things, but I think you misjudge the kind of friends we are. The kind of friendship we have."

Hamilton grunted. "Misjudge? I was in the Marines. I fought side-by-side with people who became my brothers and sisters. We went through shit together. Hell, you know? You want to talk about a bond? A friendship? These people were closer to me than actual blood. Forty-three brothers and sisters, with a sergeant who was like our father. That's tight. That's family. And when we each got out after we'd served our time —yeah, some re-upped, but not all of us—we all said the same things you guys probably have said to each other. Let's keep in touch." She shook her head, and looked down at the tarp. "Doesn't happen. Maybe you stay connected on Facebook, you know? Like posted pictures on Instagram? In real life, though? You're alone."

"You're not alone," Neeson said.

"You know what I mean," Hamilton said.

Tymere and Marshall stamped through the forest back into camp, thankfully drawing everyone's attention. Marshall parted the netting with the back of his hand and held it aside for Tymere.

"What did we miss? Seems like—what's going on?" Tymere asked.

"Just talking about graduation," Natalie said flatly. She moved over some on the mat for Tymere. He dropped down next to her. She pulled a small bottle of hand sanitizer from her backpack and squeezed out a few drops into his palms.

Marshall moved over toward Hanson's makeshift table. "What are you guys looking at? Is that the map?" Marshall looked at Michael.

"Making sure we are headed in the right direction for tomorrow," Michael answered. He wanted the map back. He felt exposed having it displayed the way it was. The last several minutes had been nothing shy of awkward. He wished he could wind time backwards and get a redo on this. He sensed animosity and mistrust from Hanson and his team. The dynamics shifted, and he worried it set them all at odds. Hanson and his team versus Michael and his friends.

"And?" Marshall asked. "Are we?"

Hanson gathered the map, reset the lantern, and then proceeded to gently fold the map into quarters. "We are right where we should be," he said. He handed the map over to Michael. "Since Albright gave us a set of coordinates to work with, we'll reach that point around noon. However, if there is treasure, as indicated on the map, it may take us a little longer to reach that specific location and find the treasure. This may add a few extra days onto the end."

"I will compensate you and your team for any additional days spent in the jungle, naturally," Michael said. The tone of the excursion had twisted. It left a rock in his gut.

"Naturally." Hanson smiled. There was nothing friendly about the expression. "It's just that we also have other engagements. We're contracted to be elsewhere by the end of the week. People are counting on our support and expertise, you see. We cancel at the last minute and word gets around. Seldom do people spread praise when a job is well done. Mess things up, and everyone who's anyone will hear about it. Know what I'm saying?"

Michael ignored the question. He got the point. It wasn't that Hanson was out of line. The man's assessment made perfect sense. The issue was, what could they do about it? What did Hanson intend to do about it?

Back when he had been in the planning stages, Michael simply considered Hanson and the guide team as mere employees. He knew *now* he'd been wrong. He couldn't shake the sudden sinking feeling overcoming all of his senses. Could this trip into the rainforest have been the biggest mistake of his life?

Hanson retrieved the collapsible shovel and toilet paper. "If I'm not back in half an hour . . . go on without me."

Reeves and Hanson laughed.

Before ducking out from the camp netting, Hanson back-tracked to his spot and, as he snatched his cell phone off where he laid his head, he and Michael made eye contact. "Have to check Facebook."

When Hanson winked, Michael held back a shudder, but said nothing as Hanson disappeared into the night.

14

They woke to the sound of rolling thunder. There was no mistaking the crack of lightning. The storm sounded as if it had snuck up directly over them. The sudden downpour allowed water to immediately pool on top of the tent covering. It wasn't long before the ground under the tarp became mushy and muddy.

Everyone pitched in to gather up the campsite, saving the taking down of the tent covering for last. As they set out on the trail Hanson created, they walked cautiously. Footing was uneven. Rocks and fallen limbs were slick. Moss and molds acted like slippery ice.

They had reached an upward slope, and the ascent was challenging. Reaching for branches for balance, and to hoist oneself upward, made the going tough. There was no time for pausing. If they didn't reach their destination, they at least needed to find a place with some cover to hunker down until the storm passed.

"I don't like being under these trees during a lightning storm," Amber said. Lightning looked for the most direct path to reach the ground. Trees became targets. It would be better, safer, if they were in a more open part of the rainforest. The wall of trees put them in danger as the storm progressed, and the number of lightning bolts in the area increased.

"We're going to be okay." Standing still wouldn't make them any safer, Michael knew. He supposed it was better that they keep moving. Hanson showed no sign of slowing, anyway. "We keep following Hanson, okay?"

She nodded, but not convincingly. As if to illustrate her fear, a bolt of lightning flashed off to the right of them, followed by a thunderous crack. Flames shot up the length of a tall tree as the base split in two. The one half fell away, crashing against other nearby trees.

The heavy rainfall quickly extinguished the flames.

"Let's keep going. Come on, now. Don't slow," Hanson called out. He had to shout in order to be heard.

Michael's body was charged with energy, adrenaline. "Keep moving," he said, prodding Amber and looking behind him to ensure everyone else had heard Hanson's instructions.

Michael was conscious of each step, worried about slipping on an uneven surface and twisting an ankle, or worse. The rain was pouring off the hood of his rain slicker. His face was wet, his hands were wet, but so far the rest of him had remained dry. He hoped his waterproof boots kept his socks and feet dry. The last thing he wanted was wet feet.

They pushed on for several hours. Michael felt a grumbling in his stomach. He was sure the others were getting hungry as well, since they had skipped breakfast. The storm put all of the planning sideways. If they were close to the spot on the map, then it made no sense stopping now. Not even if only to eat.

Michael assumed they weren't covering nearly as much ground as they expected to cover. The going was slower than expected. He didn't think they would reach their destination by noon. He couldn't dwell on it. Instead, he went back to watching each step his feet took, making sure each time he planted a foot, he wasn't going to lose his balance and fall.

Michael listened to the fast beat of his heart, and his steady, heavy breathing. The flat, muffled sounds almost echoed in his ears. There was also the sound of his arms swinging back and forth, and the rain slicker rubbing together from the motion. It was a rhythmic pattern, but far from anything musical.

He tried not thinking about time, or distance.

He concentrated instead on his walking. The side of the hill, or mountain, they scaled was gradual. However, they were gaining altitude. They were ascending higher.

Michael wasn't sure when, but the thunder and lightning had eventually slowed, then stopped altogether.

The rain persisted, but it was not nearly as bad as it had been when they started the hike that morning.

Michael saw Hanson had stopped walking. The guide stood on a ridge, looking out at . . . something.

"Will you take a look at that?" Hanson whistled.

Michael stood beside Hanson and took in what captured Hanson's attention. They had reached a small break in the forest. The visible grey sky above them was the proof. About two hundred feet across from them was thick green ground cover, however, directly below was a raging river. Large rocks peppered the water, causing the gushing river to jut and veer, twist and turn, picking up speed along the way.

"The heavy rain," Hanson said. "Could be an overflowing river or stream. Might be more of a flash flood. Either way, that is going to be a monster to cross. Over there, though, do you see it?" Hanson asked.

The others joined the two on the edge of the ridge. While the river caught their attention, it wasn't what held it.

On the opposite bank a thin outline, a shape, was apparent amid the trees, green leaves, red and orange wild flowers, vines, and roots that protruded up from the saturated ground.

"Is that what I think it is? Is it, like, a pyramid?" Natalie asked.

"It sure as shit looks like it," Reeves agreed.

"I thought those were Egyptian and Mayan things?" Neeson asked.

"Actually," Tymere said, "archaeologists have discovered pyramids similar to the ones in Egypt all over the world. Greece, Italy, Sudan, Mexico, China, Cambodia, Peru. They've even discovered some in the U.S."

"Pyramids?" Neeson said, not attempting to hide the doubt in his tone of voice.

"Peru is part of the Amazon," Hanson pointed out.

"Oh, I know. In the Peruvian Amazonia. They call them the Pyramids of Paratoari. The Dots. A NASA satellite discovered the pyramids from outer space. This was back in nineteen seventy-six." Tymere held onto a tree and leaned forward only inches, doing all he could for a fraction of a closer look. "But I don't think that is a pyramid, per se."

"Per se?" Reeves laughed.

"What do you mean, Ty?" Michael asked.

"Kind of hard to tell from here, from this distance, but over there, the stone blocks? And that might be an entrance through all of those vines, there?"

"I see it," Michael said.

"You mentioned a temple, right? Your father did, right? There is kind of a pyramid shape, a point to the top. But with all of the overgrowth, I would wager this is more, or was more, of a place of worship, rather than a tomb for dead rulers," Tymere explained. "I can't wait to get a closer look. Even from here—see the symmetrical shapes? And the spacing between the formations? Damn. This keeps getting more exciting by the day."

"So," Neeson said, "not pyramids."

"I'm not saying that. Could be. Temple. Pyramid. I suppose we'll find out soon," Tymere said. It seemed as if he were talking in his sleep, as if he were the only one on the ridge looking down at the temple, or pyramid.

"Actually, *even* from here, I can see they are perfectly placed stone-cut blocks. We haven't run into any of the locals yet, but I surmise they are primitive?" Tymere shrugged. "Bare chested. Loincloth cinched around the waist? I'm picturing bamboo huts, longhouses? Spears made from sharpened bones on the ends of sticks?"

"Don't forget frog-poison dipped tips on the ends of arrowheads," Hamilton added.

"I mean, am I wrong?"

"The deeper you get into the jungle, the more . . . primitive. Yes, that would be an accurate assessment. There are large groups of tribes that have little to no contact with us civilized people," Hanson sneered. "And your point?"

"We're talking about people who, for centuries and maybe longer, have lived in longhouses that have been basically slapped together with mud, branches, and tree bark, right?" Tymere said, and shrugged a second time. "So, who built the temple down there with precise engineering, cutting and shaping rock? Moving blocks that probably weigh more than a ton and set them one on top of the other. That's all I'm saying."

"So, if not the natives living in the Amazon, then what? Are you talking about aliens?" Hamilton asked. "Like intergalactic intelligent life from outer space? Some green or grey beings who came down here and showed a bunch of primitive civilizations how to build . . . what? Pyramids? How in the hell would that temple benefit a superior lifeform? I can answer that question for you. It wouldn't. So why would aliens waste their time teaching, or even doing the building themselves, if it didn't somehow serve them?"

"I'm not discounting anything," Tymere said, refusing discouragement. "I'm just saying, how could diverse civilizations across the globe design and build almost identical structures, without some kind of shared knowledge or insight? How could the natives living in this rainforest manage an incredible, durable structure like that? With what tools?"

"So, you do," Hamilton scoffed. "You mean aliens?"

"Think whatever you want," Tymere said. He didn't sound offended. He almost didn't seem to be blinking at all. His eyes never stopped exploring the area around the hidden temple. "I wonder if it's a tomb or, perhaps, a place of worship?"

"What if there is a curse? Like a mummy curse?" Neeson asked, laughing.

Was he joking, though? Michael wondered. Michael looked at everyone for a moment. "And that, everyone, is the reason we're here. Hopefully, the answers to all of our questions are down there. Waiting. Way I see it, there's only one way to find out!"

"If I were a pirate, and I came across something like that temple, or whatever it is that you want to call it, *that's* exactly where I would hide my treasure," Hanson said.

"Have you ever seen anything like this, like that structure?"

Hanson shook his head. He never looked away from the temple. "I have heard stories about these pyramids peppering the Amazon, but I've never come across one. The thick tangle of leafy vines, the fallen trees over it, around it . . . the place is pretty well hidden. We could as easily have walked past it if we were looking specifically for it. You have to wonder, though. Has it been abandoned for hundreds of years, or covered up the way it is by design, to look abandoned?" Hanson said.

"How are we getting across the river?" Natalie asked.

"I don't think that is a natural river," Hamilton said. "My guess? It was a brook, or stream. All of the rain created something of a flash flood. A major flash flood, I suppose."

"How deep do you think it is?" Marshall questioned.

"We're not walking across that." Hamilton shook her head. "Step on a slippery rock, lose your balance, you'll be swept miles downriver before anyone even has a chance to notice you're missing."

Suddenly, the muddy ground where they stood gave way.

The earth crumbled under their feet. While the others jumped back, Michael and Amber reached for each other as they tumbled down the embankment toward the fast flowing, muddy brown water.

Amber screamed on the way down.

PART THREE

When there is no turning back, then we should concern ourselves only with the best way of going forward.

Paulo Coelho

1

It took a split second before Michael understood what had happened. They stood on the edge of the ridge. The day of heavy rains softened the earth. Without warning, the ground gave way. A chunk of the embankment carved from the rest of the land. The severing was silent, not like when a mountain of ice cracks and falls away from an iceberg into the ocean.

Michael's arms shot up and then out, reaching for any handhold. Amber, who had been standing beside him, was falling as well. They grabbed onto each other, which was of no help. The two of them had the ground drop out from under them and went tumbling down the side of the cliff toward the swift, raging water below.

Michael heard Hanson shout: "Get back! Everyone, get back!"

Exposed, long, entwining roots jutted out from the side of the ridge wall. Left handed, Michael was able to take hold of one. He held onto Amber with his right.

The motion of falling stopped. Michael found himself face to face with the embankment. It felt as if his right arm were being ripped out of the socket at the shoulder. "Hang on, Amber!"

"I won't let go," she yelled. "I'm not going to let go."

"Try to climb back up over me," he ordered. He shifted his waist around, attempting to dig the toes of his boots into the mud.

"Don't move," Hanson shouted down from above. Michael chanced a look up. He saw the guide securing a rope around his waist.

The root Michael had clung onto gave. Michael dropped half a foot. "This root isn't going to hold us much longer!"

"Stay still," Hanson said.

"Amber? Amber, can you get your feet on anything?"

"I'm trying," she called up to him. "Don't drop me."

"I'm not going to drop you," he promised. "Are there any

other roots you can grab onto?"

"I don't want to let go of your arm."

She had his arm in both of her hands. The combined weight of their hanging bodies was too much stress on the root. It wasn't going to snap, but it was pulling free from where it had been safely buried within the earth forever.

Michael's grip on the root was numbing. He couldn't feel his palms any longer. Every instinct in him wanted to re-grip the root. If he did so, they would fall into the river. Of all the potential dangers facing them, Michael never expected something like this. "Are there any roots or anything you can hold onto?"

"I see some roots."

Something tickled the back of Michael's left hand. He looked up, and let out a shrill cry.

"Michael?" Amber called.

A large, dark orange centipede, with black legs, had emerged from where the root jutted out from the embankment. Its legs ran across the back of his hand. It stopped scurrying when Michael cried out. It stood on many of its back legs, its head hovered around above the long, flattened body. The front antennae wiggled back and forth, as if tasting the air.

Michael thought he once read certain Amazonian centipedes were venomous, but couldn't recall exactly. It had something to do with the forelegs. He couldn't remember. He stayed as still as possible.

"Michael?"

With his teeth ground, lips barely moving, Michael said, "Just give me a second here."

"Mike?" She tried again.

A little louder, Michael said, "Give me a second, please."

As if deciding Michael was no threat, the front end of the centipede lowered its head back down. The antennae passed over the hairs on the back of Michael's wrist, perhaps this time tasting him. And then it continued on, the rest of its body coming out of the dirt. The centipede had to have been around ten inches long.

Only moving his eyes, Michael watched the creature escape the embankment as it climbed over other roots and disappeared into a hole in the dirt.

Michael realized he had been holding his breath. He exhaled. It came out as a long, loud sigh. "Bugs, I get all the bugs. I hate bugs."

"Michael?"

"I'm okay. I'm okay. Roots. The roots by you, tug on them!" He knew he was yelling. "Will they hold you?"

Michael kicked at the earth, and managed to fit his toe into a hold. It took some of the tension off his left arm. Not much.

A length of rope unrolled alongside Michael. He looked down and saw the end of the rope reach the river below. A moment later, Hanson rappelled down the embankment and stopped next to Michael. His feet were flat on the embankment. He looked as if he were sitting on a harness of ropes.

"Get Amber first," Michael managed.

"Naturally. I am going to quickly tie this around your waist. Stay as still as possible." Hanson moved fast, hugging a rope around Michael. The sizable backpack and rain slicker made the effort more complicated. However, the guide expertly tied off a taut-line hitch knot, wrapping one end through the loop around Michael's waist twice, then creating a new loop, and fitting the end through there. Hanson pushed the knot, like a tightening lasso, around Michael's back. "Other end of this is around a tree, okay? You're not going anywhere. Now, hang tight."

"Oh, that's funny," Michael said, as Hanson lowered himself further down the embankment. Michael wasn't sure how much longer he could hold on. As if in an illustration to the strain inflicted, the root once again gave, dropping him another few inches.

"Michael!" Hanson shouted.

"It's not me! The root—it's giving out. It's not going to hold us much longer!" Michael knew he was panicking. His eye twitched in an uncontrollable fashion, like a tick.

"And it doesn't have to. I've got Amber. That will eliminate a lot of the extra weight."

"Hey," Amber shouted.

"You know what I mean," Hanson answered. "Now, Michael, be still!"

"I can't do it," Michael heard Amber announce.

"You have to trust me, Amber. Okay? Let me tie this rope around you. Just like I did with Michael, okay? Stay still. Keep still for a minute."

There was a moment of silence. Only that wasn't accurate. Michael could hear the anger in the river. It sounded stronger than before. It was almost as if the water wanted its due sacrifice, and was getting pissed he and Amber were close to getting rescued. The river was all he heard. He imagined monkeys and birds and jaguars perched in trees around them, silently watching the drama unfold.

There was only the churn and growl coming from the river.

And then the weight pulling on Michael's right arm was gone. "Oh, God, no!"

"I've got her, Michael. She's safe," Hanson assured him. "Now, walk up the side of the cliff with me, Amber. We're going to do this together."

"Walk?"

"That's right. Lean back a little. Your friends have you. They won't let you fall. Trust them, and trust me." Hanson sounded calm and in control. "That's it. Just like that. Plant your feet—exactly, just like that. Good. Good."

"Okay," she said.

Hanson hollered, "We're going to start back up now!"

Michael still held onto the root with his left hand. His right arm was above his head, his hand holding the rope in a white-knuckle grip.

"Cross one hand over the other and walk with me back up to the top. Okay? On three. One. Two. Start walking."

It was less than three minutes when Michael watched Amber walk up the cliff. She was focused. She chanced a look over at Michael. Her mouth opened a little. She didn't say a word.

"You're doing great, Amber!" Michael encouraged her. "Keep going. Don't stop! Get to the top of that hill!"

Directly behind and under her was Hanson. He looked like climbing mountains, and abseiling off rock faces, was as natural for him as playing a video game was for Michael.

A sudden sensation, like shame, flooded over Michael. What had he been doing with his life? Sure, he was in college, and always got good grades. He had no idea what he wanted to do with his life, with his future. What he did know was that he had been wasting days. Going to movies, watching TV shows, spending hour after hour playing video games . . . Hanson might make him feel apprehensive at times, but there was no denying how skilled at *life* the man and his team actually were.

They spent their life living. They didn't spend day after day doing next to nothing.

It was a bit of an eye opener. Albeit, an eye opener at an oddly placed time. But wasn't it when life hung in the balance that a person contemplated . . . life?

This was a part of Michael he suddenly knew he didn't just want changed and improved upon, it was something he knew needed all of his attention. If he made it out of this mess alive.

It seemed silly, a single rope away from plunging into a river, but he made a vow. From this point forward, he was done with his old ways. Done. He wanted more out of life, out of his life. All these years he should have been demanding as much.

His father spent decades . . . living. Had Michael been a disappointment to his father? Had his father hoped Michael would have shown more interest in . . . everything? Something? . . . Anything?

As painful as it was to acknowledge, to admit, he was certain of the answer. It hurt, but he knew he couldn't hide from it. He would, however, see to it that everything in his life changed.

"I'm sorry, Dad," he whispered. His forehead pressed against the dirt.

"Ready, Michael? We're going to pull you up, now." Hanson shouted over the edge of the embankment. "Try helping as much as you can, okay? Your feet, your legs. Okay?"

"Okay! I'm ready." *God, am I ready.* "Let's do this!"

2

They spent a good half hour at the top of the embankment, away from the edge, making sure everyone was all right. It was agreed they should break for lunch. Not particularly hungry at the moment, Amber and Michael shared some water.

Marshall shouldered Michael. He whispered, "Not to make light of what happened, but I am pretty sure I got the whole thing on the GoPro."

"We almost died," Amber said. Michael knew she was still a bit shaken. He was, as well. He kept an eye on her. She was the one with all of the medical experience, but what worried him most was shock. He knew the basic signs to look for. They were all present. Amber struggled catching her breath. She was shivering. Most obvious was an almost faraway look in her eyes.

"Yeah," Michael said. "Not now."

"Well, let me tell you," Marshall said. "When the edge of that hill fell out from under the two of you, I thought my heart stopped. But not Hanson and his guys. They dropped their bags and removed ropes. They were tying knots, and securing the rope to trees, and then the next thing I know—*Bloop!*—Hanson, he's *dropping* off the side of the cliff after you guys. I don't think any of them said a single word. I mean, they might have? But there was this . . . cohesiveness to their movement. Like a damned ballet, is what it was. Graceful, swift, and smooth!"

"You two should force a little food down." Hanson walked up behind them. Michael wasn't sure how much of Marshall's rendition the guide overheard. Hopefully, Hanson missed the part about the GoPro.

"You both burned off a ton of calories. We skipped breakfast, and we've been hiking for hours. Food's going to help you build up your strength. Give you some energy."

"I feel pretty wound up right now," Amber said. She held out a hand. It trembled.

Michael refrained from checking if there was a quiver in his hands. He was almost certain it would shake as bad as Amber's, or worse. There was no reason everyone gathered around needed to see him shaking like a leaf.

"Adrenaline will do that," Hanson said. "I assure you, when that settles down, the two of you are going to be starving. We have to get across that river. The temple you've been looking for is right on the other side. If I know you guys at all, I know once we reach the temple we're going right in, yes?"

Michael nodded.

"Okay. Then eat something. Who knows when we're going to sit down to a delicious meal like this again. Might not be until late tonight. By then you both will be dragging ass. We have no idea what other challenges we'll face today—"

"He's right," Amber said. "It took all the strength I had just to hold onto your arm while we were dangling over that river. A minute longer, and who knows? I might have had to let go."

"You wouldn't have let go," Michael said. He wasn't sure he was being honest. Truth was, both of his hands had gone a little numb. His muscles ached. A minute longer and maybe he'd have had to let go, too. "But you're right. Let's eat."

Michael was either, in fact, starving, or the MREs were starting to grow on him. He ate everything inside the pouch with relish, finished his water, and had to admit he felt a little refreshed, rejuvenated.

"Okay," Hamilton said. "I'm ready."

Michael stood up, leaving his MRE pouch behind. "Wait. Ready? Ready for what?"

Angelina Hamilton stood by the thick tree where the rescue ropes had been secured. Her gear sat on the ground, her rain slicker draped over her backpack. She had her gun strapped around her waist, the holster resting on her thigh. Michael hadn't noticed her muscular figure before, but it was clear and visible in her tank top as she checked the durability of the rope fastened around her mid-section. She reached behind her head and took a section of ponytail in each hand and pulled, ensuring the band holding her hair in place was tight. "I'm going back down, and across that river. Only way we're all getting from here to over where that buried temple is if we zip line to the other side."

"Zip line?" Amber got up onto her feet as well, the rest of

her meal forgotten. She took a few steps forward and stood beside Michael. "You mean you want us to cross *over* the river?"

"That's exactly what she means." Hanson double-checked the knots on the rope around the tree, and then tugged on the rope fastened around Hamilton's waist. He walked closer to the edge of the embankment and chanced a look over. "She is going to rappel back down the side *here*. Work her way across the river, and then climb the tree right *there*." He pointed at a tree across from the one Hamilton was tied to. "She will secure the opposite end of this rope to that tree, at a lower point, obviously. And voilà!"

"Voilà?" Amber asked. "That doesn't sound easy. Have you guys looked at how fast that river is flowing? What if she falls in? How would we even get to her in time to save her?"

Hamilton grinned. "I'm not going to need saving, but I do appreciate the concern."

Michael thought the idea of a zip line stretched over the river was absurd. It didn't sound safe at all. He did not wish to put his friends at further risk. Every turn of the journey had brought about unforeseen dangers. What was sold as a fun getaway before their senior year in college had become a constant dance of utter mayhem. "No one has to go across if they don't want to. Since I am assuming we have to leave a lot of our personal belongings behind, it actually makes sense to have a few people stay back and keep a lookout on things."

"Just be sure you roll up the windows and lock the car doors," Reeves added.

"What's that supposed to mean?" Tymere asked.

"I'm just saying, Albright over here is implying this is a rough neighborhood."

"Well, isn't it?" Tymere asked.

"A jaguar jumps out of one of these *here* trees while you are, so called, protecting the gear, what are you going to do about it?" Hamilton asked. She walked backwards toward the edge of the embankment, her hands on the rope, keeping it taut from the tree with each step backward she took.

Michael wasn't sure how to respond. Hamilton brought up a good point, one he couldn't answer. None of them, other than, probably, Hanson and his team, had ever encountered a jaguar.

Michael knew from his father's journal jaguars had been a threat when he last came out to the Amazon looking for the same treasure, the exact same hidden temple.

"Still," Michael said, finally. "If anyone wants to stay with our things, you can."

"I advise against that," Hanson said, in an almost insistent tone of voice.

"And I am giving my friends that option."

"You tasked my guide team with keeping all of you safe on this twisted expedition. If your friends choose to separate from the group, I have no control over their safety any longer," Hanson said.

"You know what a dead tourist does to a Yelp rating?" Reeves chuckled, until Hanson held up a silencing hand.

"Enough," Hanson said.

"I'm going with you," Amber said. "We've made it this far. On the other side of that river is something that maybe no human has seen in centuries. I'm all in."

"You sure?" Michael asked. He had been most worried about her. She struggled with crossing the rope bridge the other day, and that structure had been pretty soundly constructed. Except for some swaying in the wind, Michael had felt quiet on the bridge. A rope extended from tree to tree, over a raging river, painted a different picture altogether.

"I am very sure." Amber nodded her affirmation with lips definitely pursed.

"Me too," Marshall said. "I know all of this has been crazy. And I might be a little touched in the head, myself. But I am kind of loving every minute of it."

"Not going to lie," Tymere added, "but I feel the same way. You told us we'd embark on some wild adventure, and you were right. I can't compare what we've done with anything I've ever done before. At the risk of sounding crazier than Marshall, I am actually looking forward to zip lining."

Michael looked at Natalie. "Nat?"

"I'm with these guys. I'm all in. Our gear will be fine without us. And if it's not, I'm betting Rambo over there knows how to survive a few days out here as we make our way back. Isn't that so, *Gregory?*"

Hanson tried not to let it show that the slight delivered had landed. The tip of his tongue did touch his top lip as he let out a near-quiet *tsk* sound. "I believe we'd make it back to the boat without these supplies, if that became the case."

Michael felt somewhat relieved. He didn't realize his friends were actually enjoying themselves. He knew he was so busy worrying, the idea of asking them straight out never occurred to him.

Quickly reflecting on the moment, Michael realized something. He, too, had never felt so alive. A plan, a future idea, grew inside him. He wished he had the time to sit and contemplate. It wasn't anything he'd forget. The object occupying his thoughts would have to wait, but the prospect of such a scheme excited him.

Like he had seen Hanson do a half dozen times before, Michael took a step forward and clapped his hands. "Well, all right then, Hamilton. Let's get you down the side of the cliff and safely to the other side."

Hamilton flashed a half smile. "That's what I like to hear. Give me a hand."

Michael followed her to the edge and, as she fixed her feet in place on the cusp of the slope, Michael picked up the balance of the coiled rope. "Come on, everyone."

Hanson stood back as Michael's friends surged forward and fell in line behind Michael. They all took a portion of the rope in hand.

"We've got you," Michael promised. He gripped, and then re-gripped the rope. This was something he had never done before. He hoped with all of them hanging onto the rope, they could easily guide her from the top of the ridge to the bottom in a smooth effort.

"You'd better have me," she said. The half-smile filled out as she chanced a look over her shoulder and down the side of the ridge. "Hold on tight."

And with that, she was gone. She dropped a few feet down. Her boots planted firmly against the muddy wall. Her weight pulled on the rope. Michael held on with all of his strength.

"You have to give me some slack," Hamilton called out.

"Right," Michael said.

Sticking their footing, they allowed some of the rope to pass through their hands and, little by little, they gently lowered

Hamilton down the edge of the embankment. "More," she yelled.

They gave her more rope. As she descended, the lot of them got into a rhythm. She bounced a few feet downward, then they tightened their grip. They provided slack, and she rappelled a few feet more before they once again tightened their grip.

Before long, Hamilton called, "I made it."

Michael looked over the edge. They all did.

Hamilton walked toward the river. All of the rain was a contributing factor to the gushing, mud-brown water. There was no sign of it slowing down. If anything, it appeared to be flooding the side banks, working its way closer to the side of the cliff Hamilton had shimmied down the side of.

Hamilton rolled up the surplus of rope, pushed an arm through the center, and rested the rope on her shoulder. She leaned forward and rested her palms on the closest, biggest boulder in the river. The water rushed around the rock, only on the furthest side, the side facing the opposite bank. The ground where Hamilton stood looked more like quicksand instead of dry land. Her boots sank deeper into the muck. She leaned her weight onto her hands and pulled free her left foot. She planted it on the rock, and then lifted the other leg.

Hamilton stood on the rock, hands on her hips, and looked around.

Michael supposed her perspective looked even more treacherous from where she stood than it did to all of them still standing safely at the top of the ridge.

The next rock jutting up and out of the water was only half the size as the one she stood upon. And the one after it was even smaller.

Michael knew Hamilton was assessing the leaps she would need to make in order to get from point A to B to C, and then, finally, onto the opposite bank. He had to bite down on his tongue to keep from yelling out it was okay to turn back.

He wondered if he would have what it took to jump across that river? One slip, one bad landing, and she would lose her balance. The rocks were wet, slippery. If she fell into the river, the current would carry her a mile away in a matter of minutes. She could drown right before their eyes.

"Be careful!" Marshall shouted. He'd had his hands cupped

in front of his face, creating a makeshift megaphone for carrying his voice.

Everyone turned to look at him. Hamilton even looked up from where she stood, perched on a rock at the edge of a crazed river.

Marshall lowered his arms, as if suddenly uncomfortable, and shook his hands. "I know. Captain Obvious. I'm sorry." He cupped his hands and directed his next apology down to Hamilton. "I'm sorry!"

Hanson shook his head. "Captain *what*?"

"Obvious." Marshall dropped his eyes and focused on his boots. "It's a thing, never mind. I said I was sorry."

Everyone still looked at him.

"What? I couldn't think of anything else to say." Marshall shrugged, letting his shoulders sag.

Michael drew his attention back onto Hamilton as she prepared to jump from one rock to the other. She quickly made sure the rope was seated securely on her shoulder. She put both arms back, and bent her knees.

Inside his head, or maybe out loud, Michael counted. "One. Two. Go!"

As if on cue, Hamilton uncoiled her legs, as if a released spring, and jumped.

Time moved in slow motion. For a fraction of a second, Michael saw Hamilton come up short. He imagined her plunging into the river, going under, and being swept away. That isn't what happened. Instead, Hamilton practically flew as she made it from the first rock to the second. In fact, she made it look easy. Michael was reminded of a gymnast making a landing at the end of an uneven bars routine. The only thing Hamilton didn't do was raise both arms in a V, in celebration of nailing the landing.

The third rock, much smaller than the first two, would be far more difficult to land easily. It also looked a bit further away than the second rock had been from the first. The rising water was starting to pass over the top of the third rock, as well. In a few moments that rock could be underwater, and then Hamilton's attempt at crossing the river would be thwarted.

"Is anyone else feeling anxious?" Marshall had both hands balled into fists. He kept them both up near his face. "I almost don't want to watch, but I can't look away."

Michael felt the same way. There was no way he could look away. Not now. It seemed like every insect and animal in the jungle was holding its breath in anticipation of her next jump. An occasional monkey could be heard, but it almost sounded as if the furry animal was cheering Hamilton on.

Like before, Hamilton brought her arms back and bent at the knees.

With nearly twice the distance to cover this time, she was going to have to exhibit a bit more spring when she leapt to the second rock. She kept looking down at her feet and then over at the next rock.

The water was definitely getting higher by the minute. The river wasn't splashing over the rock, it started passing over it consistently, constantly. The time to make the jump was now, or the opportunity would most certainly be lost.

Before Michael could shout out something stupid, like, *Don't do it*, she launched herself from one rock onto the other. Her arms pinwheeled. Her body bowed forward, and then leaned backward. Her left foot slid to the side. Hamilton put her arms outward, making herself look like a letter T. Her bobbing and weaving stopped. She stood up straight.

"Whoa-*who*!" Marshall cried out.

Tymere, Amber, and Natalie were clapping.

Michael sighed, realizing he had been holding his breath. His shoulders were hunched up and every muscle in his body had been tensed. He tried relaxing, slowed his breathing, but it didn't help.

Hamilton was far from safe. She had one last jump to make before she was on the opposite side of the river bank.

"One more jump to go!" Marshall yelled. He slowly turned to look at everyone else. He held up both hands in surrender. "I know. I know. Captain Obvious again."

Yet, he was correct. One more jump. Michael knew he would breathe easier once Hamilton was safely on the other side. And then it would be their turn. Crossing the river via a Jerry-rigged zip line.

Where Hamilton stood, the river water now ran over her boots. The rock she stood on was completely submerged. Michael worried if she waited too long, the current would overpower her and knock her off-balance into the river.

If she didn't hurry, she would find herself in a seriously dangerous situation. Not as if jumping from rock to rock hadn't been insane all along. Michael shook his head. His racing thoughts overwhelmed him.

As she had done two times previously, Hamilton brought her arms back, bent at the knees and, without any countdown Michael could surmise, she went for it.

Uncoiling, Hamilton's arms shot up into the air as she sprang forward, exploding into the air and across the remainder of the river.

The toes of her boots hit solid ground on the opposite bank. But she was angled wrong. She was leaning backward.

Again, her arms pinwheeled. She never regained her balance and, instead, fell backwards, plunging into the river.

"Angelina!" Neeson cried out, and raced for the rope tied to the tree. Hamilton was still tethered. Neeson grabbed on to the end of an already taut line. It was as if the raging river threatened to strip the rope off Hamilton's body.

Michael couldn't shake a memory of a time he went fishing with his father. He'd been just a boy. His bait attracted a big mouth bass. The fish put up a hell of a fight. His stringy arms could barely control the rod. His father either saw him struggling with the fish, or he'd yelled for help. Either way, what he remembered was his father standing behind him. Together, they tugged on the pole and cranked the reel. Slowly, but surely, the fish tired out, and they scooped the bass up with a net.

They could pull her out of the river! It was a great idea. The others moved as one, following after Neeson. Michael hated the next thought the second it entered his mind. *Or recover her body.*

3

Angelina Hamilton's last jump brought her to the opposite bank, but not close enough. She fell back into the river and was at risk of drowning. Thankfully, she still had the rope for setting up the zip line secured around her waist. Everyone on top of the ridge grabbed a hold of the rope. Struggling, they attempted pulling her out of the river and to safety.

She had been underwater for an unnaturally long period of time. No one gave up; if anything, they all pulled on the rope with more determination. Neeson stood at the front of the line, feet planted in mud, veins popping on his forearms and by his temples on his forehead.

Hamilton's hand shot up from beneath the water. She slammed it down on the grass on the bank. Her fingers dug into soft earth for a hold. A chunk of mud gave way. Her hand dropped back into the water.

Fishing with his father, Michael knew what they needed. A net. There was no net.

Michael let go of the rope and ran to Reeves' backpack for another rope. It was the last one. He fastened one end around his waist.

"Mike, what are you doing?" Amber cried.

"She's getting tired." He talked while he tied the other end of the rope around the closest tree he could find. "She's been under a long time. She doesn't have much strength left."

As Michael backed up toward the side of the ridge, Amber said, "What do you think you're going to do?"

"She needs a hand, someone to fish her out," Michael explained, and without giving Amber, or anyone else, a chance to try to stop him, Michael decided he would rappel down the side of the embankment.

He realized this would be far different from falling off the edge of the ridge, like he had earlier. This time he would be in more control of the situation. Although, he had absolutely no idea what he was doing, other than attempting to mimic things he'd seen in movies, and on YouTube, he knew it couldn't be that difficult.

Reminding himself, he thought, *Try staying in a sitting position, an L shape, with my feet flat against the embankment.* Michael knew he could work out a rappelling rhythm.

Without any more delay, he started down the embankment full of confidence.

The fatal flaw was realized a fraction of a second later, as he dropped fast. There was no one up top lowering him. He had a rope around his waist, and wasn't belted into an actual harness designed for rappelling.

What he imagined he could do, and what he was actually doing, were night and day. In his mind, he envisioned Army-like precision, bouncing off the embankment and lowering himself inches at a time. In reality, he was flailing, except he had both hands on the rope. His legs kicked wildly, as if he were trying to wake from a nightmare and was wrapped up in the bedsheets.

He didn't care. He was doing it.

"Help him!" Michael heard Hanson shout.

At what felt like rocket-speed, he shot down the side of the embankment. His heart hammered away inside his chest.

All at once, the quick descent came to a jerking stop. The rope dug into his burning palms. He face-planted into the embankment mud. The wind didn't get knocked out of his lungs, but he *definitely* let out an audible *Oomph!*

It wasn't fear propelling his adrenaline, though. This time it was purely a sense of . . . *drive.*

When his feet hit the ground, he bent forward. Hands braced above his knees. He breathed in and out for a moment. "That was stupid. That was stupid," he whispered.

"You okay?" Neeson stood at the top of the ridge, looking down at him.

Michael flashed an *okay* with a hand gesture. "You did it, though. You did it."

He stood up straight, untying the rope from around his waist. The river was at least fifteen feet wide. There was no way he could just reach in and fish her out. He thought about throwing her the end of his rope, but unless she was looking for it . . .

She wasn't completely under water. She was more or less on her back, her head above the surface. She gasped for air as water rushed over her head, as if she were a rock.

The only way to help her was for him to reach the other bank. The only way across was the path Hamilton tried, and failed at. If he stopped and thought about it any longer, though, he'd never work up the courage to attempt the crazy thing he was about to do. Upriver, the oddly placed rocks and boulders churned the swift raging river into a frenzy of whitecaps and froth.

He leapt from the bank onto the first rock and, without pause, onto the second rock.

He ignored Amber shouting for him to stop, to go back. It wasn't too hard. The river demanded all of his attention. It sounded as if he were bouncing around inside a continual clap of thunder. The roar was nothing shy of deafening.

He knew right where the third rock was. The water had risen over it, but it still caused a flux in the waterflow. He stood in the middle of an out of control river. The water level continued rising.

He sucked in a deep breath and then jumped to the third rock, landed with his left foot, and immediately launched himself for the river bank. His arms stretched out in front of him. His chest landed on the ground. The lower half of his body splashed into the water. The current pulled at his legs. His fingers scrambled for something to hold onto. He did an army crawl, pulling himself up onto a bent forearm, then pulled himself forward.

Once his waist was out of the water, he knew he had made it. There was no time for giving thanks. Instead, he pulled himself up and onto his feet. He ran down river and dropped onto his belly at the bank, thrusting an arm toward Hamilton.

She took hold of his wrist, and he gripped his fingers around her wrist. She suddenly let go of the rope altogether, and her other hand grabbed him by the arm. Her fingernails cut into his flesh.

Wincing, he pulled her toward him, rolling his body away from the bank for leverage.

He heard people cheering before he realized half of her body was out of the river. Without letting go of Hamilton, Michael repositioned himself. Sitting, he ground the heels of his boots into the saturated earth and fell backwards, hoisting Hamilton all the way out of the river.

She coughed and gagged, turning onto her side.

Michael crawled over to her, placed a hand on her shoulder, and moved wet hair off her face. "You're going to be okay."

"You saved me," she said.

"You would have done the same for me," he replied.

Coughing, she brought her knees up, and Michael patted her on the back. "You wait here. Okay?"

Michael gathered together the rope. He knew the goal. They needed to get everyone else safely across the river. The tree on this side of the river looked easy enough to climb. As Hamilton had done, he wound up the slack in the rope and fit the coil over his shoulder.

Taking hold of branches above his head, Michael pulled himself up and into the tree. He lifted a leg and straddled the nearest branch. Wrapping the rope around the tree, he started tying the rope in the best knot he could muster.

"The rope has to be tighter!" Hanson shouted from the ridge on the opposite side of the river.

Michael untied the rope. He pulled on the end as hard as he could, before wrapping the rope around the trunk a few more times. This made attempting another knot more effective.

He tested the tautness of the rope with a finger pluck. It was a pretty solid attempt. The rope didn't strum tight like a guitar string, but he figured it should be taut enough, especially because Hanson wasn't still shouting at him.

"Good job."

He looked down. Hamilton stood below him. "How are you feeling?"

"I'm fine," she said. "That's a good angle, too. About four percent. You stay put, keep an eye on your knot."

"Okay."

Hamilton turned and faced the others. "Okay! Start over!"

It looked as if Reeves was coming over first.

"How are they going to do this?" Michael asked.

"They'll attach a carabiner on the rope, and then something through it to hold onto, a belt, a shirt. Something they can secure their grip with," she explained.

"That doesn't sound safe," Michael said.

"Impromptu," Hamilton said.

Reeves walked up to the edge of the ridge. His canvas belt had been pushed through the carabiner, and then he cinched it around both of his wrists before stepping off the ridge.

The carabiner slid smoothly down the rope and, within seconds, Reeves landed on the other side, joining Hamilton. They hugged each other tightly. He heard Hamilton tell him over and over she was okay.

They finally separated and turned to encourage the others.

One by one, first Marshall, then Natalie, and Tymere, joined Hamilton and Reeves on the bank on the opposite side of the river.

Michael could only imagine Amber's anxiety level. Crossing the bridge had nearly crippled her mentally. He knew she was a strong person. Soaring over a river with a piece of clothing through a carabiner was not going to sit well with her.

And yet, she stepped up to the edge of the ridge.

"You got this," Michael mumbled. He almost couldn't watch. He wanted to squeeze his eyes shut. There was no way he would chicken out. If she was going to do this, he would observe her heroics from start to finish. He would not miss a second.

On the ground, the others called out encouragingly.

In his head, Michael counted back with her. Three. Two . . .

She lifted her legs, as opposed to stepping off the ridge, and gravity took over. Unexpectedly, she cried out, "Hell, yeah!"

Michael's eyes grew wide, watching her . . . smile? Was she enjoying the zip lining? She was! She was actually having fun.

Tymere and Reeves reached for her waist as she passed the river and was safe above the ground. She dropped into their arms.

"Okay, that ended up being quite a rush!" she exclaimed, giving Michael two thumbs up.

He had never felt more relieved.

Without incident, Neeson and Hanson made their way across.

Michael unhooked each carabiner and dropped them down to the others before he climbed down from the tree.

"We made it! I can't believe we all made it," Michael was

saying, as he brushed his palms over his pants. No one moved. They resembled statues. They stood still, staring off into the distance, an almost vacant expression on their faces.

Michael followed with his eyes in the direction they all were staring.

Almost hidden by the cover of large plant leaves, he saw what had captured their attention.

Marshall spoke for all of them. "Who the hell are they?"

4

On the edge of the top of the embankment stood four people. Three men and a woman.

"Gregory Hanson," Michael said, as he turned away from those standing on the ridge. "What is going on here?"

"Who are they, Michael?" Amber asked. She shifted her weight from one foot to the other, as if unsure how to stand. Clearly, she was trying to assess the situation.

"Hanson?" Michael insisted.

Hanson rolled his lips under his teeth and bit down. "Just to be clear, you paid my company a fee to get you from point A to point B. Which we've done."

"What?" Tymere said. "What the hell is going on?"

Michael pointed at the grey-haired man standing beside the young woman. "That man right there was my father's old partner. Nicholas Katic."

Katic looked disheveled compared to the debonair man who had shown up at his father's funeral. The last time he'd seen Katic, the man wore a sleek black suit with silver cufflinks, and polished Italian shoes. His hair had been slicked back and it was near impossible not to notice such perfectly manicured fingernails. Katic currently looked as if standing up straight made the muscles in his lower back spasm. The curator's shirt was untucked, and his hair was wild in wisps branching out in all directions.

"What's this all about?" Tymere asked. "Mike, what is he doing here?"

Hanson waved the others over. The two men, dressed very similarly to Hanson and his team, helped the woman onto the makeshift zip line.

"What are they doing here?" Michael asked. "Hanson?"

"They paid us to follow you, and a bonus if we gave them a lead at the point just before discovering the treasure." Hanson looked over at the temple covered in shrubbery and shadows. "I believe we have reached that point."

"You sold us out?" Marshall said.

Hanson folded his arms. "Not at all. As I explained, Mr. Albright here paid us to get him through the Amazon to this point. Which we've done."

"That is shi—"

Michael put his palm against Marshall's chest, silencing his friend. "So you knew about the treasure the whole time?" It made sense. Hanson showed little curiosity about the specifics of the expedition. It had nothing to do with professionalism.

Amber took Michael's hand. "So why are we just standing here? Let's get into the temple first. We can get a good head start while they struggle getting across."

Reeves pulled his sidearm. He leveled it at Michael's chest. "Not how this is going to work. I'm sorry."

Michael stared at Hanson. "You're sorry? Really?"

Hanson shook his head. "Reeves is sorry. I'm not. There's nothing to get upset about. This is business. If you feel strongly about this, I highly recommend reporting us to the Better Business Bureau when you get back to the States. A bad review from the likes of you will certainly harm our operation, what with the tourist season coming up soon, and everything."

Hanson laughed as he threw his head back.

Michael had never been in an actual fist fight. Every instinct inside his body flared with anger. He was tempted by the idea of throat punching Hanson, but refrained. The idea Reeves still had a gun pointed at him had little to do with the reason why he did not.

Michael and his friends were herded close together and forced to stand quietly while the four interlopers zip lined across the river. The surge of the water had decreased. The banks less flooded, and the river slowly began to resemble a stream. The floods from the heavy morning rain must have subsided.

Once across, they started toward Michael and the others. The two crewmen working for Hanson walked a few steps behind Katic and the woman.

"Mr. Albright," Nicholas said. He used the back of his forearm to swipe sweat off his brow. "Things did not need to work out this way. I tried—"

"You tried?" Michael interrupted the curator. "What are you talking about? You wanted one of my father's maps. I wasn't interested in the offer. So you followed us? You think you can swoop in and finish what my friends and I have started?"

"What *you* have started?" Nicholas laughed. He bent forward with hands on his knees and laughed. "Michael, you didn't start anything! You didn't start all of this. What you think you know is far from the truth."

"The truth? I have no idea what you're even talking about. What truth? It is my father's map. My father's. That's the truth." Michael felt every muscle in his body tense. He clenched his teeth. This entire scene felt surreal.

"That, Michael, is the problem."

"I don't understand any of this. And I certainly don't understand you, Mr. Katic. I wish you and," he waved flippantly at the woman, "you and her would reconsider this escapade and let us finish our adventure."

"Your adventure. That is too cute. Really, it is. Your adventure."

"Mr. Kat—"

"Do you want to hear the truth, Michael? Will you allow me that little grace?"

Michael spun around, stopping at a face-off with Reeves. "See this, Mr. Katic? Guns. He has a gun pointed at me. He has had it pointed at me for almost an hour now. When you say allow you a little grace, I would have to say I am not in the mood for such allowances."

Nicholas Katic looked at Hanson. "I don't think the weapons are necessary at this point. Do you?"

"It's your rodeo," Hanson said. He waved a hand at Reeves, who holstered his sidearm. "See?"

"See?" Michael said using a mocking tone of voice. "You paid off my guides. Overpaid them. That's what I see. I've been bamboozled."

Marshall said, "Bamboozled?"

"Not now, Marshall," Michael pleaded in a hushed whisper.

"Can I tell you a story?" Katic asked. Without waiting for a response, he continued, "Just before you were born I came here to the jungle with your father, and my brother. Jeremy."

"Mr. Katic, with all due respect," Michael said, holding up

his hands and shaking his head.

"With all due respect, Michael, shut the hell up," Nicholas said, a bite in his words. His face reddened and spittle pooled in the corners of his mouth. "Let me continue without interruption."

Michael was taken aback by the outburst. In reality, they were in danger. The armed guides had proved untrustworthy. They were literally in the middle of nowhere. Things couldn't get much worse.

"Your father did the research on the pirate's treasure. He found sections of the map in old, old documents and pieced it all together. The man was a genius when it came to that kind of work. We had gone on many, what did you call them? Adventures? Yes. We had gone on many adventures together, but on this one things got bad fast. We were only a day into the jungle when our team was attacked. First by jaguars, and then by natives. Unfortunately, a jaguar killed my brother. Rosemary's father. Jeremy."

The woman beside Nicholas Katic lowered her eyes. Her body stood rigid, though. "Father," she said.

"It's okay." Nicholas reached over and patted her on the arm. "I have raised her as my daughter. She was a baby, an infant, when we came out to this jungle. Rosemary's mother was never very healthy. My wife and I took them both in. That is what family does. That is what I did."

Michael looked at Amber. She narrowed her eyes, as if unsure what to make of it all.

"I am sorry about your brother, your father, but I don't . . ."

"Your father was in love," Katic continued. "When he returned home after the nightmare of our . . . adventure, he married your mother, Pricilla. Not long after, she was pregnant and I knew Alexander was done. He was out."

"Out?"

"Treasure hunting. He gave up. And why wouldn't he? He had made a fortune. He wrote books. He spoke at colleges, making more in a few hours than I made in a year. You don't know how many times I begged him to sell me his maps, or to go on one last adventure." Katic snickered. The humorless sound came out more sinister than anything. "I had a wife, Rosemary, and Rosemary's sick mother living with me. The bills mounted, Michael. Mounted. And still your father wouldn't sell me the map, any of his maps."

"He wrote in his journal about why he left it all behind," Michael said. "He wrote about your brother's death. It tore him apart."

"Someone your father knew died out here looking for this treasure? The treasure we're now looking for?" Marshall asked. "You knew about this? You knew it was so dangerous that your father, an experienced treasure hunter, gave it all up and vowed not to return here?"

"I knew." Michael locked eyes with Katic.

"And you brought all of us out here?" Amber asked.

"Marshall almost got eaten by a snake, Michael," Natalie said. She held Tymere's arm in both of hers. She clung to her boyfriend.

"I wouldn't say eaten," Marshall added.

"If I may?" Katic held up a finger. "You can have your turn berating your friend in a moment. He and I are kind of in the middle of something here."

"You know, I get it, Mr. Katic," Michael said. "You think the two of you are somehow entitled to the treasure."

"My father died working for *your* father, and he received nothing in return for giving his life. Nothing." Rosemary stared at Michael with ice in otherwise bright blue eyes.

A silence fell over everyone. Michael felt conflicted. It had nothing to do with Nicholas Katic. He couldn't believe his father would have left Jeremy's widow and infant with nothing. He had no way of confirming any part of the story right now, though. Not while they were out in the middle of a jungle.

"So, what are we doing, Mr. Katic?" Hanson asked.

Michael spun around. "Seriously?"

"Our business is concluded for the moment, Mr. Albright."

"What about getting us out of here?"

"Are you ready to go back?" Hanson asked.

He wasn't. "No," Michael said.

"Then, for the moment, we are under the employ of Nicholas Katic."

"I would like to make one more attempt, Michael. We work together on this."

"Meaning what?" Michael asked.

"Fifty percent of the findings goes to Rosemary. The remaining fifty percent we split equally," Nicholas Katic proposed.

It was never about fortune, Michael knew. He also knew now was not the time to start an argument. Whether he agreed with Katic or not, the best course of action was to agree. Give in. Let him think he had won.

They were outnumbered. The odds were stacked against them.

Rejecting Katic's offer in front of Hanson could prove detrimental. He tried not letting his actual feelings show. He kept the anger buried, and his frustration masked. This would not be the end of negotiations, just the end while they all stood out in the middle of the Amazon.

Michael looked at each of his friends; he hoped they knew he was not a coward, or merely giving in. Each, in turn, nodded approval. Slight nods, but nods just the same. Tymere's left eye twitched. Michael was certain the two of them, at least, were on the same page.

Reluctantly, Michael said, "We agree."

Nicholas Katic looked stunned. Rosemary allowed herself to smile, and looked almost relieved.

"May we shake on it?" Katic asked.

"If you insist," Michael said, and stepped forward. "Now what do we do?"

Katic, for the first time, turned around and assessed the pyramidal mound. "I suggest we find a way inside this glorious relic of a temple!"

5

Gregory Hanson and his team sat back and watched while the others worked machetes against the overgrowth that must have covered the pyramid for, perhaps, centuries. The blades *thwacked thwacked thwacked* at thick vines and lush green leaves.

Michael's body was covered in sweat. He stood near the top of the buried pyramid and hacked away at anything and everything that wasn't stone. Stripping the structure bare felt like an impossible task.

The work went on for close to two hours, until Tymere shouted out a find.

"Guys! I think I found an entrance." Tymere stood back, fists on hips and his machete askew in one of his clenched hands.

Michael made his way down the side of the pyramid. It was like climbing down from the mast on the rope rigging of a large pirate ship.

The others had already gathered around Tymere by the time Michael reached the ground. He brushed himself off as he made his way over.

Michael caught something out of the corner of his eye.

A half-naked man. Bare-chested, the indigenous native with dark red skin was wearing a jaguar pelt loincloth. One end of his spear was planted on the ground, the sharpened blade, white as bone, pointed upward toward a lead sky which promised more rain. There was nothing threatening about his stance.

The idea of seeing natives in the Amazon was something Michael spent plenty of time thinking on. After watching documentaries on television, and reading articles in National Geographic, he'd formed an impression of the indigenous in his mind. Not once had he expected to feel fear when confronted by the people.

Here was just one, probably curious, man who did little

more than watch them from a higher vantage point, and yet, Michael's legs felt cemented in place. Similarly, the tribal man—with a spear—had not moved a muscle. The two of them stood perfectly still, staring at one another.

"Michael?" Amber asked.

Michael backed away. He kept his eyes on the native. There did not appear to be any threat. Michael thought he'd write it off as mere curiosity … for now. There was enough tension in the group with Hanson and his crew.

Once Michael saw the progress Tymere made on the side of the pyramid, he nearly forgot about the man in the loincloth. Nearly. Tymere had certainly discovered what could very well be a passageway, rocks stacked inside of a cut-out entrance.

"Think the way in is behind those rocks?" Natalie asked.

"Only one way for us to find out," Amber said, as she slid her machete into the sheath on her hip. Without delay, she reached for a rock and removed it, then threw it as far to the side as possible.

Everyone followed suit. For the next half hour they removed the smaller rocks with ease, and then battled the larger boulders together, rolling them away.

"You think there was a reason why the entrance was sealed with rocks that way?" Marshall asked.

Nicholas, still catching his breath from the laborious work, nodded. "Curses," he said.

"Curses?" Marshall asked.

"It wasn't uncommon for natives to believe temples like this were cursed," Rosemary explained. "Especially if someone important was buried within. If this was designed as a tomb, the only way to scare off raiders was by placing a curse on the pyramid. Then the rumor would spread around. Anyone that entered the tomb would bring something like death to their family, or plagues to the community. That kind of thing. A curse."

"That's what I thought you meant." Marshall sighed.

Rosemary continued, "Curses, and magic, and mythology was widespread and believed among ignorant people who didn't have the science to understand natural phenomena, like eclipses, and earthquakes, and volcanic eruptions. Those occurrences sparked fear into people, and the only explanations they could come up with were angry gods. That's where sacrifices and the like were bred. A way of appeasing an angry entity."

"Sacrifices," Marshall said. "*Go on an adventure*, Michael said. *It'll be fun*, he said."

"What . . . What are you doing?" Natalie asked.

"Bruce Willis? Die Hard?" Marshall shrugged in a matter of fact fashion. "Never mind."

"I don't get it," she said.

"Well?" Amber said. "Are we going in?"

"We most certainly are," Katic said. "The lanterns."

Everyone retrieved an LED lantern from their backpacks, moving with a bounce in their step. Michael felt his exhaustion fall away, replaced with optimistic apprehension. Standing back and looking at the pyramid-shaped temple, at least at the spots where the machete had provided a view into the construction, he was simply amazed. He took it all in for a moment, letting questions fill his mind. The visible stone foundation looked like giant, perfectly-shaped rectangular blocks. Where had those blocks of rock come from? How had they been moved to this remote location? How had one been stacked on top of another? The feat of building a temple in these conditions seemed an impossible undertaking, yet here he was, standing at the foot of such a monument.

For a moment they stood in front of the entrance, no one moving. Michael caught Marshall adjusting something on his vest. He knew it was the camera, and was thankful his friend continued recording their journey as documentation. The footage might prove helpful once they returned home, if Katic tried any more funny business.

"Well," Michael said. "Let's do this. Let's go in and see what we find."

Katic held up a hand. "Rosemary should go in first."

Michael bit the inside of his cheek. "Of course."

Amber squeezed Michael's hand in silent protest.

The situation still felt volatile. Michael did not want trouble. If there was an opportunity to turn the table, he would take it. Right now, he didn't see any other way around things. Katic and his niece held the cards. They had the upper hand. For the moment, anyway.

Rosemary looked hesitant for a moment. Then she stepped

forward, passing through everyone. She ducked her head and disappeared through the narrow passageway. Her body blocked the light from the lantern she held out in front of her, and it was as if she vanished.

# # #

Once inside the temple, the floor was more like a slick ramp leading down into the belly of the earth. The temple did not stand tall in the midst of the jungle, but it seemed as if the bulk of the structure was below ground.

The stone walls dripped water, and were slimy to the touch. Michael, who was ahead of Natalie and Tymere, heard the two of them talking in whispers.

"I am not great with tight spaces," Natalie said. "When I was, like, eight, I slept over at my aunt and uncle's house. With all of the cousins. There were five of us altogether. And while I wasn't the youngest, I was the first to fall asleep. We had sleeping bags spread out all over the living room. On the floor. On the couches. Well, my cousins thought it would be funny to push my head into the sleeping bag, roll up the end, and hold it closed. It didn't help with how dark it was in the bag, but there was really no room. I could barely struggle. I mean, I tried kicking and screaming, but it was as if all the air was squeezed out of the sleeping bag when they rolled up the opening. I thought my lungs were on fire. My arms were stuck at my sides, and all I could do, it seemed, was kick my legs."

Tymere asked, "When did they finally let you out?"

"It felt like I had been trapped inside the sleeping bag for hours. Hours. It was maddening. In reality, it was all of probably a minute or two. Ever since then, you know, I kind of hate enclosed places."

Tymere said, "You should see when we go through a car wash--"

"Don't make fun of me."

"I'm not. Not at all. I'm giving some more definition to how serious your claustrophobia is. When we ride into a car wash, she clenches her muscles, eyes closed, and she sings along with the radio until we get out on the opposite end. It's that drastic."

Amber was directly ahead of Michael. "How are you doing?"

"It's so dark. The walls are so wet. I can feel the dampness in my bones," she said, not sounding at all like she was enjoying the experience. At this point, was anyone?

"It is definitely cooler inside here," he said, and shivered as if illustrating his point. The shiver raced down his spine. The hairs on his arms stood on end. He hoped it wasn't an omen.

"I see something ahead. I think it is an opening!"

It was Rosemary. She must have reached the end of the slope.

"Oh my goodness," she said. "It is. It's an opening!"

Michael felt his heartbeat race. What did she see? He couldn't wait to reach her. Everyone seemed to quicken their steps, shuffling forward. Still cautious, Michael wanted to push forward. Slow and easy was the safer route. They seemed cursed, speaking of curses, stumbling into dangerous situations.

With the exception of Amber performing CPR on Marshall, no one else had been seriously injured. Michael wanted to keep it that way. The biggest danger no longer existed in the jungle. Not anymore. Hanson and his goons were what concerned Michael most of all.

He no longer trusted Hanson, if he ever really trusted him to begin with.

Michael knew he had to bide his time, wait for an opening, and then . . . and then what? Attack? Hanson and his para-military platoon were lethal, carried weapons, and knew the jungle inside and out.

Fear filled Michael. He felt his heartbeat quicken, and sweat bead on his forehead, as he realized the awful truth—some of them might not make it out alive.

6

Rosemary and her uncle stood side by side at the mouth of the chamber. They had all followed a narrow, wet and damp tunnel, which descended deep beneath the small temple aboveground. Michael could not gauge how far below ground they actually were, though.

The chamber itself couldn't have been much larger than a twenty by twenty square-shaped room. The walls appeared to be cut and stacked stone. At the opposite end of the room stood a waist-high stone wheel. It looked out of place. Perhaps there was a potential doorway behind it? If there was a doorway, it was half the size of the one they had walked through. Crawling on hands and knees might be the only way into that next, unknown, tunnel-way, if, in fact, one existed at all.

If there was no other passageway, and this was the only chamber, then there was nothing. No treasure. No fortune.

Natalie's breathing made Michael apprehensive. She sounded close to hyperventilation. He knew the tight confines of the tunnel they passed through triggered her claustrophobia. Thankfully, Tymere did his best to keep her anxiety in check.

"Just focus on your breathing. In. Out. Nice, slow, even breaths, okay?" Tymere kept one hand on Natalie's shoulder, the other was on her arm above the elbow. Natalie listened, and followed his directions. Amber kept an eye on her friends, as well. If Tymere offered bad advice, Michael knew Amber would have given alternative directions. Since Amber hadn't said a word, Michael figured Tymere had things as under control as possible.

Marshall, on the other hand, wore a giant smile. The man appeared to truly be enjoying himself. He sucked in a deep breath, puffing out his chest. When he exhaled, he let out a squeal. "Let me tell you what. The air inside here is stale. I feel like we walked into some party balloon that had been blown up a century ago by some ninety-year-old person."

"Great comparison, Marsh. Just wonderful." Michael lifted the collar of his shirt over his mouth and nose. He hoped the cotton fabric distilled the putrid, uncirculated air inside the chamber. The LEDs illuminated the room, highlighting newly disturbed and kicked up dirt as it now floated through the air, as if a thin, rolling wave of dust.

Hanson moved about the chamber, unimpressed. "It's empty. There's nothing here. A big rock."

A stone, Michael thought. *A wheel, actually.*

Nicholas Katic walked along the wall opposite from where Hanson stood. Michael watched as Katic ran his hand over the stone blocks. "Hmmm," the curator mumbled.

Unable to help himself, Michael asked, "What? What did you find?"

Katic, as if startled by the sound of Michael's voice, spun around. "Hmmm? Oh. Well, I just find this curious."

"What's curious about a wall?" Hanson asked.

"Not the wall. The mortar used between the mortar joins. The masonry work is, well, remarkable!" Katic looked around the chamber, like he expected someone else to concur.

Tymere left Natalie's side and walked the length of the wall Katic had walked, also skimming the cut stone with his palms.

"Do you see it?" Katic sounded like a college professor grilling one of his students.

Tymere nodded and pulled his hand away from the wall. He stared at his fingers, rubbing them together. The way Tymere cocked his head to one side and wrinkled up his mouth and nose, it looked like he might be tasting the wall with his fingertips. "The mortar is gypsum, with some charcoal and wood."

"Yes," Katic agreed. "The charcoal and wood would have been part of the heating process. The kindling, so to speak."

"What is gypsum?" Amber asked.

"A soft sulfate mineral," Tymere explained.

"It is widely mined and used as a fertilizer," Katic said.

"And, as a mortar for building," Tymere added. "A very similar compound was used for, like, the construction of the pyramids in Egypt, Ancient Rome . . ."

"Medieval England . . . the Byzantine Empire!" Katic proclaimed, as he waved hands about.

"Mesopotamia? In Western Asia!" Tymere's eyes were wide in astonishment. Michael witnessed his friend's excitement. The energy around Tymere was practically visible. It wasn't everyday Tymere had an opportunity to shine as he showed off his personal archaeological interest. Right now, Michael had to admit, Tymere resembled a brilliant scholar, even when going toe-to-toe with the likes of the curator, Nicholas Katic.

Tymere and Katic grinned at one another, coming close to matching the smile still worn by Marshall. They were like children who spoke their own language, twins reunited after years of separation. Their excitement was almost contagious.

"These places, Hanson waved a hand around, which resembled him trying to scoop up everything the other two were throwing down. "What does Egypt, Asia, and England have to do with this temple?"

The curator let his brow furrow in surprise and, maybe, distaste? Michael felt relieved Hanson asked the question, because he had no idea what Tymere and Nicholas Katic were ranting on about, either.

"They used a similar mortar for construction." Katic shook his head. "It's fascinating to get this close and touch the temple walls the way we are. Like the chubby one said earlier, the air tastes a century old, at least."

"Chubby one?" Marshall pointed at himself. His broad smile fell askew toward one corner of his mouth. "I like to think of myself as more the big boned variety. Maybe something of an underlying thyroid issue."

Amber patted Marshall's arm. "You're not heavy."

"He could stand to lose a few," Katic said.

Marshall gripped the spare-tire area. "I mean, he's not wrong."

"Silence!" Hanson made fists at his sides. His body shook. "Does the gypsum mortar have anything to do with finding the treasure?"

"The treasure?" Katic repeated. "Why, heavens no. It's remarkable being some of the first people in over a hundred years to explore the craftsmanship of an otherwise undiscovered ancient temple in the heart of Brazil, don't you think?"

"Then I suggest we keep moving forward." Hanson ushered everyone toward the opposite end of the empty chamber.

Natalie pointed at the small doorway. She shook her head. "I'm not going through there. I'll wait for you here. I'm going to stay right in this room." She held out both of her arms. She looked like a child playing airplanes. She backed around the chamber, looking left and right, making sure extended arms didn't touch anyone.

"It's going to be okay." Tymere attempted to calm Natalie again. His serene tone of voice didn't do the trick this time.

"Sorry. It's not." Hanson gave a curt nod towards his crew. "We're all going through. No one stays behind. We can't protect someone if the rest of us have moved on."

Natalie's body quivered. She looked like she might start crying. She brought her hands up to her mouth. "I'm not going through that. You can't make me."

Hanson pulled his sidearm out of the holster and pointed the weapon at Natalie's head.

Tymere jumped in front of Natalie. He spread his arms wide. "Hey! What do you think you're doing?"

"Lower the gun, Hanson!" Michael crept toward Hanson. "You have to stop pulling guns on us."

Amber and Marshall moved fast, blocking both Tymere and Natalie with their own bodies.

"Not another step, Albright." Hanson changed aim. The barrel looked centered on Michael's chest. "If you haven't figured it out by now, the game has changed."

"Who's playing a game?" Marshall asked.

"Gregory, what in the world are you going on about?" Katic asked.

Rosemary looked like a coiled snake about to spring against a threat. She was half crouched in front of her uncle. "What are you talking about? My father hired you to do a job."

"Technically, I hired him first," Michael said.

"Didn't keep his word with Mike," Marshall said, "I'm kind of shocked the two of you are now surprised he isn't keeping his word with you."

Dismissing Marshall's one-sided banter, Nicholas cleared his throat. "Greg, we have history. You've been on expeditions with me before. I've always treated you and your team fairly."

"Fairly?" Hanson snickered. "Define fairly. On all of the runs we've made together, both you and Albright's old man made a fortune."

"You think I made a fortune?" Katic asked.

"You did very well for yourself, yes," Hanson said. "But what about me? What about my team? We still have to scrape up money to purchase supplies, repair engines . . . feed our families!"

"And how is that my fault?" Katic asked.

"How is it *not* your fault?" Hanson retorted.

"Let me see if I have this right. I tell you about a job, and all it entails. You give me a price. I agree to pay that price. You complete the job. I pay you. And you see that as me doing you and your team wrong?" Katic laughed, clearly amused. "If you wanted more, why didn't you ask for more? Had I ever haggled on a price with you? And for this particular trip, I offered you a large sum for a payment, and you readily agreed."

"It's not the same thing," Hanson defended his position.

"I should say it isn't. You and I both knew Michael Albright was also paying you. You greedily accepted, because in your eyes you were double dipping. Getting paid more than twice the normal rates for technically one job. The same job. But you're mad at me, at Michael's father, because you made poor business decisions? I hardly see how that is any fault of mine, or ours— Mr. Albright and I."

Hanson leveled his weapon. Without warning, he fired. Everything happened fast, but unrolled in a slow motion Michael would never be able to explain, or forget.

A splash of fire erupted from the barrel of Hanson's gun. The deafening sound of the gunfire assaulted Michael's ears. Everything sounded muted and muffled as the bullet slammed into Katic's chest.

Katic's body didn't fly backwards like people getting shot in the movies.

A patch of blood spread over Katic's shirt.

The curator stood like a statue for several seconds, in the midst of a cacophony of screams bouncing off the stone walls of the chamber, before he started toppling forward.

Michael smelled what he assumed was gunpowder, a pungent nitroglycerin odor. Everyone held everyone else back, except Hanson and his crew. They looked hungry for any scrap of confrontation.

Rosemary turned and faced her uncle, gripping his arms and sinking with him, guiding him down into a kneeling position on the dirt-covered stone of the chamber floor.

Amber kept Michael at bay.

Tymere grabbed a protective hold of Natalie, moved her behind him, and backed both of them up into a corner of the chamber furthest away from Hanson.

Marshall dropped onto his knees, opposite a crying Rosemary, and planted his hands on Katic's shirt. His palms became submerged in blood that bubbled out of the hole in Katic's chest.

Amber made sure Michael wasn't going to do anything foolish before she rushed to Rosemary's side. Michael watched as she placed two fingers on Nicholas Katic's neck, by the throat.

Amber looked up at Michael. In that brief moment, he knew. There was nothing more she could do.

The look in Katic's wide-open eyes told him all he needed to know, as well.

"There was no pulse," Amber said. "I'm sorry."

Rosemary let out a feral roar and stumbled as she tried lunging toward Hanson.

Hanson raised the weapon.

Amber fell over Rosemary, knocking her to the ground. Amber covered Rosemary with her own body. "No! No you don't!"

Hanson's team—Reeves, Hamilton, Neeson, and the other two who had accompanied Katic and his niece through the jungle—had sidearms drawn. Aimed. Stern, unfazed expressions spoke volumes. They were a command away from killing everyone.

Michael knew this could turn into a bloodbath, a massacre, at any moment. Michael waved his hands. He surrendered for himself, for all of them. "Stop this! Please, stop! Just . . . stop!"

"Leave him." Hanson waved his gun toward the large round stone. "Let's get that moved out of the way. That has to be blocking a passage into another chamber. Come on! You two."

Tymere and Michael looked at one another.

"Yeah," Hanson shouted. "The two of you. Get to it."

The slab of round stone was smooth. Solid. Michael and

Tymere stood on one side. The stone, wide enough so they could both fit their hands on it, let them set their footing as they pushed. The stone must have been in place for as long as the temple had been around. It didn't want to budge.

Grunting, Michael thought the stone might have given up some ground. "I felt that."

Tymere nodded his head. "I did, too. I felt it."

"Keep pushing!" Hanson ordered.

Michael was not doing any of this for Hanson. He also wanted, needed, to find out what else might be contained, buried, deeper within the temple.

Straining, and worried vessels in his temple might explode, Michael gave moving the stone everything he could. His arms shook, and his legs threatened to buckle.

The payoff was the stone rolling along the wall, toward the corner of the room, and the revelation of another passageway.

Hanson clapped his hands together. He let out a low, soft whistle. "Well, well, well. What do we have here? It is another tunnel. And if I were a betting man, which I am, I would bet most anything that the treasure we're all so eagerly hunting for is . . . that-a-way! Alright now, why don't our friends go on ahead first. Don't you worry now, we'll be right behind you."

As they shuffled toward the small tunnel in the wall, Amber guiding Rosemary forward, Michael knew none of them would ever see the light of day again.

7

Gregory Hanson ordered the two crew members, the ones he never bothered introducing, to pass through the tunnel behind the rolled away rock first. They did not require much prodding. They shared an LED lantern and scurried through the passageway like kids playing a game of hide-n-seek.

Natalie wanted Tymere to enter the tunnel next, with her directly behind him. Tymere bent forward so he would not bang his head on the archway and low ceiling. It was better than having to crawl, Michael supposed. Natalie grabbed onto the back of Tymere's tactical pants and vest, and charged ahead. Michael imagined she had her eyes closed, maybe hoping it would lessen the anxiety of her claustrophobia attacks.

Marshall followed behind Natalie, while Amber stayed close and helped Rosemary. The woman seemed to be in shock. Her hands trembled, quivered. Michael knew it could be some time before Amber had a chance to fully evaluate Katic's niece.

Michael went last. Without looking back, he knew Hanson and the balance of his crew filed in directly behind him. It made him very uneasy. He did not like having his back to them. He had never wished more for eyes in the back of his head. Michael's mind spun around and around in a whirlwind. He knew there had to be a way out of this mess. He wasn't sure how, though. Not when they carried semi-automatic weapons, and he and his friends were only armed with machetes. While the blades were indeed sharp, and could prove useful, deadly even, he didn't think the machetes would match up against a bullet. Not to mention, Michael didn't trust his survival instinct.

The idea of swinging a machete at another person terrified him. He wasn't sure he could even do it. It didn't seem to matter that this had become a life and death situation. He supposed shooting someone was far less personal than stabbing, or hacking, another person. The sinking sensation of steel piercing flesh, the vibration as the sharpened edge skidded across bone . . . Those thoughts, in the heat of the moment, might cause hesitation.

Hesitation would get him and his friends killed for certain.

That was the problem with revolting. Uncertainty. Hesitation. Fear.

He felt ashamed by his pause.

And then his thoughts were halted as he emerged on the other side of the passageway.

On each wall was a makeshift sconce. Someone, more than likely one of the two from Hanson's crew, had lit the ends of the mounted torches. Bright firelight made the shadows in the room come alive and dance.

The lanterns, set on the ground around a singular stone coffin, highlighted the painted, golden lid. The artwork depicted a young woman, adorned in jewels, with large round eyes. It did not resemble any of the Egyptian sarcophagi Michael had seen in museums he'd visited with his father over the years, or the ones he'd seen in books and photographs. The craftsmanship was equally breathtaking, and the depiction a few brush-strokes shy of lifelike. Overall, it, nonetheless, captured some remarkable semblance of a long-ago ruler of some tribe that may have once lived in the Brazilian jungle. The Amazon's own Cleopatra? Hatshepsut?

"A sarcophagus," Tymere whispered.

Solid gold relics—chalices, bowls, a staff with a red jewel mounted at the top—were stacked in the four corners of the room. Under the sconces sat gold statues of children with wings, in various poses of playfulness. The overall shrine might have been meant to please the one contained within the, as of yet, undisturbed coffin.

They had entered an ancient tomb, a sacred burial temple.

At the foot of the stone coffin, Michael saw a small wooden box. It was the one item which clearly appeared out of place among the other valuable pieces. Michael wondered if it was, in fact, the chest that spawned the journey in the first place.

It must be the treasure hidden by Roche Braziliano. Michael was almost certain of it.

The wooden box from the 1800s looked less preserved than

the artifacts surrounding it. Badly warped wooden slats bore rusted hinges and front and center latch. The bulky key lock appeared as if one good smash with a rock would suffice, and the secured away contents concealed inside would be revealed. Michael felt his heartbeat race, despite the gloom and doom of the circumstances. They had actually done it. He wished he could tell his father what they had found. Hell. He wished his father had been with them.

No! Not with them. Not with Hanson and his crew about to kill them all and steal the treasure.

The treasure chest was irrelevant. The prize inside did not matter.

This was about his friends, and getting out alive.

"Michael, you and your friends are to get against the back wall." Hanson waved a dismissive hand at them. "Face the wall. Line up. Get on your knees."

He would shoot them in the back. This couldn't be the end.

"Don't make me ask again. This is your one chance at living through all of this. Do we understand each other?" Hanson's tone of voice sounded anything but generous, or sympathetic.

Michael gathered his friends, and Rosemary. He silently ushered them to the back of the tomb.

"On your knees. Lace your ankles, one leg over the other. Do it," Hanson ordered. "Hands behind your heads. Now!"

Reluctantly, Michael and the others complied.

Hamilton walked behind them, and as they reached and faced the stone wall, she removed the machetes from each scabbard. Michael noticed the loss of weight on his hip immediately. It reminded Michael of the way he felt when he'd gone to class but forgot his cell phone in the dorm room. He despised the sudden naked and vulnerable feeling. His indecision about taking action was stripped away.

Any chance for surviving had now completely dissipated.

8

Michael and the others were on their knees, facing the back wall of the tomb. They had their legs crossed at the ankles, and hands behind their heads. Behind them, it sounded as if Hanson and his crew were removing everything of value from the crypt. After about an hour, Hanson clapped his hands as he had done dozens of times before. "Mr. Albright. Mr. Albright. Mr. Albright."

Michael wanted to turn around and face Hanson. He remained where he was, on the ground, his nose less than an inch from the stone wall.

"This is where we must part. It has been our pleasure," he said, and laughed. "And I thank you for all of your assistance, and the map. Of course, I thank you for the map. I, my team and I, finally can retire from working as servants to people like you and your father."

Michael found it hard to believe. This was the end.

"So you're just going to kill us?" Michael asked. They needed closure. Even if moments before imminent death.

"You think I am some kind of heartless murderer?" Hanson sounded genuinely offended.

"You killed my father!" Rosemary cried out.

"I think we all learned today that he was your uncle. That right there is some sordid shit, let me tell you."

"You murdered him!"

"He wasn't going to stop! He was going to keep at it!" Hanson lost his cool. His voice boomed in the now near-empty chamber. "There was no other option. He sealed his own fate."

"And us?" Michael attempted regaining some form of control over the conversation. This was their last chance. Weaponless, the only tool Michael possessed for defense was his words. "So what's the plan? You are going to let us go? We stay like this. We are no threat. You guys take off, we'll stay right here overnight. You have our word. In the morning, we'll find our own way out of the jungle. None of us ever have to see each other again."

Hanson burst out laughing. "Sure, Mr. Albright. It's something like that."

"What do you mean? What does that mean?" Michael asked. He felt the conversation slip away from him. "Something like that? Something like what?"

"You heard Katic's daughter." He over enunciated the word daughter. "She thinks I murdered her father. You all think I did."

The nail in their proverbial coffin. Hanson couldn't afford to let them live.

"You said you weren't going to kill us. You said you are not a murderer. We're good with that. We all believe you," Michael tried.

"You killed my father," Rosemary shouted.

"Not now, Rosemary," Michael hushed her.

Hanson laughed again. "Look, I am not planning on killing any of you. Not even you, little Ms. Katic. What I want you to do is exactly what you said. You stay still. You face that wall. No one turn around. Okay? We understand each other?"

"We get it. We understand each other." None of it made sense. With his nose to the wall, it was impossible to look a gift horse in the mouth. He had no idea what that even meant. The expression popped into his mind. "We're not going to move," he assured Hanson, and then commanded the others, "No one move. No one turn around."

Michael didn't want Rosemary unleashing another outburst of accusations.

Their best bet was letting Hanson leave and worry about the next steps after.

For a long moment, only the crackle from the burning torches could be heard. That changed when something like the sound of crunching gravel filled the chamber.

"Mike, they're sealing us in here!"

Michael spun around in time to see Tymere stumble backwards, trying to get to his feet.

"Ty, wait!"

The stone rolled in place, blocking their only way out.

The tomb became deadly silent.

Michael imagined Hanson clapping his hands in the other ante-chamber. *Welp. Let's get out of here*, was probably what he told his crew.

"Mike," Amber said.

"There is no way they removed everything from the tomb," Michael said.

"So what?" Natalie asked. "What difference does that make?"

"They probably just moved it from here to the other small chamber," Michael explained.

"I'm not following you," Tymere said.

"That means we have at least another hour in here. Maybe after they remove the relics outside of the temple, they will roll back the stone door." Michael shrugged.

"And maybe they won't," Natalie said.

Rosemary paced back and forth. She kept her fists planted on her hips. "He's right," she said, almost as if she were talking to herself.

"Right?" Amber asked. "Right about what?"

"Let's say we can roll the stone out of the way, then what? If they are still removing the artifacts from the other chamber and we pop in . . ."

Everyone seemed to comprehend the significance all at once.

"So, Hanson was giving us a chance to get out of this, as long as we sit tight."

Michael nodded. "Exactly."

"What about the torches?" Marshall pointed at the walls.

"What about them?"

"Who knows for sure how long we'll be here? Fire eats oxygen. This room seemed pretty well sealed. The stagnant air. We could suffocate if we let those flames burn up all of our air for breathing," Marshall explained.

"We do have the lanterns," Natalie pointed out.

"Okay. Good call. Why don't we put out the torches," Michael said. If they were trapped inside the tomb, the oxygen burned up by the torches didn't really matter. If there was no air in the room, they would suffocate eventually, regardless.

Tymere bent forward and started down the tunnel.

"Ty?" Michael called out.

Ty stuck his head back into their tomb. "I want to see if I can hear anything. That's all."

"Don't try moving the stone wheel," Natalie warned.

Michael didn't think they'd have a chance in hell moving that wheel. Best he could tell, it was somehow tethered to the wall. Rolling it away had been difficult when he and Tymere moved it earlier. That had been while standing, using leg and back muscles, and really putting their weight behind the challenge. "Just be quiet, okay?"

"Not a sound," Tymere said. "Not a sound."

After several minutes, the group couldn't keep still. Michael felt cabin fever immediately set in.

Amber comforted Natalie. He supposed Natalie's anxiety from claustrophobia creeped in. Perhaps she slowly accepted their strangled fate as a real possibility?

"What are we going to do next?" Marshall whispered. With no one else talking, it didn't matter. He might as well have screamed the question out loud.

"We are going to get out of here," Michael said.

"That's great," Marshall said. He did not sound convinced. "How?"

"When Hanson and the others are gone, we'll roll away the stone—"

"How? It must weigh a ton. Like, literally. Inside that tunnel, bent forward? You can't get any leverage—"

"Marshall—"

"—You won't have anywhere to grip it—"

"Marshall, hey! Stop it."

"I'm sorry. I'm sorry."

"Okay. It's okay." Michael gripped Marshall's arms. He gave his friend a shake. "We're getting out of here. Okay? We are going to get out of here."

Before long, Tymere returned.

"Well?" Michael asked.

"I can hear them in the other chamber. Barely, but they are there. Definitely making trips removing everything from the temple." He brushed off his hands on the thighs of his pants. "I say we give them, like, another half hour, go back and listen, and if it sounds good, then we make a break for it."

"Yeah," Michael agreed. "I like that plan. Everyone?"

They all nodded as Tymere moved in, taking Amber's place beside Natalie.

"I would like to say something."

Rosemary stood in a corner of the room, an LED lantern at her feet. The brilliant light lit her up as if she stood on some kind of altar.

"I am sorry everything went down this way," she said. She looked at her feet, not making eye contact with anyone. "Growing up, my Fathe—my uncle . . . he told me story after story about the adventures he went on with Alexander. Your father, Michael."

Michael had also heard countless stories from his own father. Many, if not all, included Nicholas Katic.

"He shared conflicting emotions. It came down to his own mood, during the re-telling, on whether Alexander was either painted as heartless, or courageous. He made your father sometimes appear generous, or selfish. There were times he told me the same story, and in one version Alexander was the hero, and in the next rendition he made your father the villain. Like I said, it all depended." Rosemary folded her hands in front of her. Holding the attention of everyone, she appeared uncomfortable, and shifted her weight from one leg to the other.

She wrung her hands together. "From the time I was little, my uncle took care of me and my mother. She has not had an easy life. She is very, very sick. My uncle has always made sure she is comfortable. He sent me to law school," she said.

"You're a lawyer?" Tymere asked. He planned on going to law school after graduation.

She shook her head. "The bar is coming up before the holidays. That's not the point."

"What is the point, Rosemary?" Amber asked. She didn't sound as if she were ready to forgive the Katics yet. Michael couldn't blame her. The two had endangered everyone, flaming Hanson's delusional conquest.

"My uncle assured me I was owed something, compensation at the very least, for the untimely death of my father. I bought into it. I believed him."

Michael sighed. "Your uncle might have been right. I don't know. I wasn't even born when all of that—when your father was killed out here in the jungle."

"I know you weren't," Rosemary said. "And I was, like, almost five at the time. I don't remember much about him. I do remember my mother and I moving in with my fa—my uncle. I remember him becoming my father-figure. I remember him keeping us safe. We never needed, or wanted, anything with him and my aunt. They took very good care of us."

"You told us this already, Rosemary," Amber said. "Your uncle was a good man to you and your mother."

"I'm sorry. I wanted to put some context around all of this."

"The problem is, when you bribed that jerk out there, you gave him the idea to rob us all. We're all in this tomb, one we probably will never get out of, because of you and your uncle." Amber's arms were stiff at her sides. Her hands were balled into fists.

Michael could not recall any time he had ever seen his girlfriend this upset. "Amber—"

"No, Michael. No. She's why we're all trapped inside here. You know it. We all know it." Amber breathed in deeply. "I'm very sorry about what happened to your uncle. I am. I think if you are trying to apologize for anything, then you are doing a really sucky job at it."

"But I am," Rosemary said. "I'm sorry about all of this."

The woman dropped onto her knees. She buried her face in cupped hands. Her shoulders shook as she cried.

Amber looked at Michael, who cocked his head to one side in return.

Amber's lips pursed, but she moved toward Rosemary. Joining the woman on the stone slab ground, Amber draped an arm over Rosemary's shoulders. Rosemary didn't hesitate, she wrapped her arms around Amber.

Gently patting Rosemary's back, but without breaking eye contact with Michael, she said, "There, there. It's okay, Rosemary. It's okay."

But was it? Was it okay?

9

Michael and Tymere sat on their knees at the end of the passageway. They sat a lantern behind them. In front of them was the one ton stone wheel blocking their one and only exit out of the tomb.

They pressed palms against the wheel, and dug their boots into the ground as best they could for a foothold and, on the ending count of three, pushed. The toes of their boots slid back.

Michael strained, felt veins in his temple throb, as he used all of his strength in a failed attempt at knocking the stone over.

Tymere stopped and clapped his hands onto his thighs. "That ain't going to budge."

Michael surrendered as well. "Not an inch. I have a feeling it is somehow secured in the wall. A, a —what do you call it— a track? The wheel is affixed. We're not going to push it over."

"Well there's no way to roll it. It's like Marshall said. There's no leverage."

Michael put his hands on the ground, and tried sliding them this way and that. "No. There's nothing."

"So we're stuck in here."

It sounded hopeless. That didn't change the truth.

When Michael didn't respond, Tymere sighed. "What are we going to tell everyone else?"

"We're not. Not yet." Michael shifted around, sitting his butt on the ground. "Do this. Back to back."

Without question, Tymere followed suit. "Now what?"

"We're going to use leg muscles. At an angle, okay? Press our shoulders against the wheel, and push with our legs. Got it?"

They pressed their boots against the walls, back to back, and Michael set his right shoulder against the back of the wheel, Tymere his left shoulder.

"On three. Ready? One. Two. Now!"

The boots gripped the wall better than the toes of their boots had on the ground.

They strained, exerting as much pressure as possible into their shoulders, but to no avail. There was zero give. The one ton stone wheel did not budge at all.

"Again," Michael stated. "One. Two. Go!"

It felt as if his thighs were on fire. Michael ignored the burn. He cursed all the times he skipped leg day at the gym.

Panting, Tymere relaxed. "It's not going to move, Mike. That thing isn't going to fall over."

"We had to try," was all Michael could say.

"We did. We tried."

Now what? Michael wasn't ready to give up. They didn't have any other options. "Maybe there's a secret exit in the tomb?"

Tymere snickered. "C'mon, man. Are you serious?"

"We push on the stones. Mess with the sconces. Maybe they are levers?"

"I think we need to go back there and have a serious discussion with everyone," Tymere said.

"I don't want to do that. Not yet. I'm not ready to give up," Michael said.

Tymere put a hand on Michael's shoulder. "We can do this, okay? They deserve the truth. Like it or not, we all look to you as our leader right now."

"That doesn't make this any easier."

And then, the stone moved.

Michael and Tymere looked at each other, and then at the stone.

Was Hanson back to finish the job? Were they all going to die. . .?

# # #

Michael and Tymere backed out of the short tunnel as fast as they could. The muscles in Michael's legs ached, felt knotted. Ignoring the strain, he scrambled backwards.

"What? What is it?" Amber asked. She jumped to her feet,

keeping Rosemary behind her. The woman was barely responsive at this point. After her confession, she'd fallen silent, become almost lethargic.

The sound of a heavy rock rolling on loose gravel filled the chamber. Someone definitely was coming for them. Michael wondered if Hanson would do it himself, kill them? Or if he would order one of his crew to complete the task.

Natalie stood side by side with Tymere. She looked ready to fight. She looked afraid, same as they all did, but also she stood ready to defend everyone. Her claustrophobia was forgotten or, at the very least, shelved for now. This better resembled the Natalie Michael knew. Fierce. "Is he back?"

Michael moved in front of everyone. His friends were his responsibility, regardless of whether they were ready to go to bat for him. He got them into this. He'd go down first, and he'd go down swinging!

From the shadow of the tunnel, a single person emerged.

It was a native. A tribal man. It might have been the same man Michael had seen when he was scaling the side of the temple earlier in the day, before they ventured inside.

Someone behind Michael shrieked. He didn't think it was any of the ladies. It sounded like it might have been Marshall.

Michael held up his hands. He did not want to fight this person.

The native stood in front of the passageway and looked around the tomb. Nothing in his expression told Michael that he even saw them. They all watched in silence as the native man walked the four corners of the chamber, his fingers tracing the stone walls.

It was almost as if he needed to touch the emptiness to verify the contents had been stolen.

"We didn't do this," Michael said, his head lowered, his hands up. "It wasn't us."

The native turned and stared at Michael. His mouth was closed tight. He breathed heavily through his nostrils. His chest rose and fell with each deep breath. After a long exhale, the man's shoulders fell, deflated. He waved for them to follow him and then disappeared back through the passageway.

"What do we do?" Marshall asked. He stood bouncing on the balls of his feet. There was no hiding his apprehension. His eyes darted about the chamber, as if he thought ghosts might start passing through the walls.

"We follow him," Natalie said, and surged forward. She ducked her head and, without hesitating, darted into the tunnel.

Michael raised his eyebrows. There was no need to voice his surprise. Even Tymere looked shocked at Natalie's brazen move. His eyes were open wide and staring at the passageway.

"We have no idea what's waiting for us out there," Michael said.

Amber said, "We know our fate if we stay here."

Everyone filed out of the tomb, Rosemary included.

In the smaller ante-chamber, Rosemary screamed.

Michael was last through the passageway. "What's going on?"

"Where's my father?" she cried. "They moved my father. They took his body!"

Michael wasn't about to argue semantics. Uncle. Father. It didn't really matter. Not anymore, that was for sure. He also wondered who took the corpse of Nicholas Katic? Had it been Hanson and his crew, or the natives? "It'll be okay. We're going to figure this out. Okay? We need to get out of this place. We need to get back outside."

"I want my father!"

Amber continued providing care. She took Rosemary by the shoulders and began whispering into Rosemary's ear. Whatever Amber said, it seemed to be working. Slowly, Rosemary relaxed some. She became calmer by the second.

"Let's get out of here," Michael said.

Natalie looked hesitant about being the first through the second passageway leading through to the temple's exit.

"I'll go first," Michael said, gently moving past everyone to the passageway. "I want everyone to stay close, okay?"

He wondered where the native had gone. Was he outside waiting to . . . Waiting to *what*? If he had wanted them dead, he could have rolled the stone back in place, locking them in the tomb forever. Except the tomb was obviously a sacred burial place for someone important to this man's tribe.

Michael held one lantern out in front of him. He moved slowly, feet shuffling forward.

He listened to the heavy breathing of everyone behind him.

Someone whimpered, holding in cries.

The expedition had become a nightmare. Sooner or later it would have to come to an end.

Michael hated thinking about the different ways the nightmare might end. And then he stepped out of the passageway and back into the Amazon fresh air.

He bent forward and sucked in a deep breath, filling his lungs, silently giving thanks. The idea of suffocating to death in a room with all of his best friends seemed like a horrible way to go.

When he stood up, the same native man stood directly in front of him.

Behind the man was a large bonfire. Giant branches had been stacked like a tee-pee, and the bright blaze crackled and roared. The fire was going good.

That didn't bother Michael in the least.

What made Michael's blood run cold was the six stakes set around the fire.

As the others came out of the temple behind him, they stood in a straight line. All of them stared transfixed by the sight before them.

The brilliance from the fire made everything else look like black shadows.

Motionless, black shadows. It was the low-growl of a repetitive chant, the unrecognizable words said over and over. Something like a drum beating in time. Not an ordinary drum, though. It sounded more like Thor's hammer was used as the drumstick.

Rosemary said, "Oh dear God."

10

The native man ushered everyone forward as they came out of the temple.

Michael's throat went dry. It felt as if his tongue swelled inside his mouth, making it difficult to breathe. There were countless natives around the fire. The men and women banged the end of spears on the soft ground, yet it sounded like thunder claps each time. The tribe moved in time with the beat of their spears, and the words of some kind of ritual chant, around the fire. The entire tribe was topless, and the flames from the fire made the painted markings across their faces and exposed bodies look illuminated. The dark skin of the natives glowed. Every single person dancing and chanting around the fire stared directly at Michael and his friends.

Chills raced up Michael's back; it felt as if a skeletal finger of ice traced along his spine. He involuntarily shivered. Dark thoughts of an inescapable and bloody fate filled his head. He saw no way out of this.

The sight of so many armed tribal natives was enough to make Michael's heartbeat threaten to burst out of his rib cage. He thought the native in front of him might even be able to hear his heart slamming away inside his chest, even over the crackling of the fire and the chant from his tribesmen.

However, it wasn't necessarily the natives that caused his body to perspire, as much as it was the six stakes set around, and closer, to the fire. This was what captured Michael's attention.

Six naked people, five men, and one woman, were impaled around the fire. It looked as if the sharp end of a shaft of bamboo had been shoved into the body, starting at the anus, and then pounded through the body. All of their heads were thrown back, with mouths opened unnaturally wide. The sharpened end of the bamboo stick jutted out from their mouths. The other end was buried into the ground deep enough that the bodies remained standing, hovering feet above the ground.

Marshall dropped onto his knees and vomited.

"That's Hanson," Amber whispered.

"And his crew," Michael confirmed. The bodies appeared as if floating in the darkness, feet dangled over the dirt and leaves of the rainforest cover.

The native who had been leading them held up a hand.

Everyone halted immediately. Michael felt thankful he did not need to take another step closer to the bonfire, or the corpses on display.

When the native whistled, the other natives circling the fire moved away from the dangerously high flickering flames, fell into a line, and then continued their dance in a procession toward Michael and the others.

The spears drummed against the ground. They almost looked like they were jogging in place. The repeated mantra became almost hypnotic. Little by little, the line of natives moved closer and closer.

Michael blinked hard several times as his vision blurred. He touched his temples, holding his head in place. He thought he might faint. The idea of suffocating inside an ancient temple sounded so much better than getting impaled and mounted.

Michael's brain raced, searching for answers, for a solution, but to no avail.

Still ready to fight, Michael attempted setting his feet shoulder width apart. He knew he didn't have the energy, or strength, to even appear as a threat to these people. Fighting to the death to save his friends sounded far better than the fate awaiting them.

Tymere grabbed his arm. "Wait. Look."

The natives weren't coming for them. One by one, they diverted to the left, where the spoils of Hanson's pilferage stood stacked beside tall trees. In a line, the natives picked up pieces from the tomb and then carried them past Michael and the others, back into the temple.

"They're returning the artifacts," Amber whispered.

Michael looked at the native man and lowered his eyes. "We were not with them." Michael pointed at the bodies around the fire.

The native grunted. "You. Go."

Go? They could leave? They were letting them go free? "Go? We can leave?"

He grunted again. "You. Go."

It was the middle of the night. Aside from the LED lanterns, they didn't have many supplies with them. It didn't matter. This might be their only chance at freedom.

"We'll go. We're going," Michael said.

"Where's my father? He was dead. Inside the temple. Where is my father?" Rosemary started shouting.

He didn't get it. This was their chance to escape the nightmare. For all practical purposes, they had been caught inside a sacred temple, and had been caught desecrating a tomb. The natives doled out punishments already, and were now being gracious toward them. They must have realized Michael and the others weren't there to steal from a grave. "Rosemary, please," Michael pleaded.

He would leave her behind, if she forced his hand.

The native approached Rosemary.

"Oh, great," Michael muttered. He couldn't leave her behind. "You guys get ready to run, I have to stop this."

The native man lifted a small leather pouch with drawstrings from off the belt around his loincloth. He uncinched the bag, lifted Rosemary's hand, palm up, and then shook the contents of the pouch into her hand.

Michael saw the black onyx ring before Rosemary closed her fingers over the jewelry.

Michael remembered seeing that ring when he was a child, and the Katics had come to their house for dinner.

Rosemary's eyes brimmed with tears. "Where is my father?"

"He is free." The native pointed toward the large bonfire flames. Michael did not want his eyes following that line of direction. He had seen enough, where he knew he might never sleep well again.

They, apparently, cremated Nicholas Katic's remains. That was the takeaway. In one sense, it was a thoughtful and compassionate act. On their part. Michael wondered if they held them blameless?

Rosemary lowered her head. She understood, as well.

The natives had handled the remains. She would not return

home with her uncle. And yet, they had removed his Onyx ring. They had saved that for her.

Michael realized people were people, regardless. He'd always considered natives living in remote jungles as primitives. They weren't. They understood more than he'd thought. Their compassion, and empathy, registered with him.

Their barbaric ritual of impalement maybe only seemed so because it was not something done in the States. Perhaps the natives would find the electric chair, lethal injection, or life in prison equally barbaric.

Impaled through the anus out the mouth, though . . .

The native man whistled.

Another, younger, man in a loincloth ran over. "Take them."

Take us, Michael wondered. Take us where?

"You. Go. Now." The native pointed into the darkness.

There was no other option. The man had given them a guide, and he wanted them gone from the temple. That much was clearly established.

"Wait," the native said. He walked over to where the artifacts from the tomb had been stacked, where the pile had slowly dwindled as tribal persons made trips bringing the relics back into the tomb. He knelt on the ground, and when he stood up, he held in his arms Roche Braziliano's treasure chest. The lock was still secured on the latch.

The native offered Michael the chest.

It weighed far more than Michael expected. The native held it with minimal effort. Michael's eyes widened, expectantly. "You want us to have this?"

"Does not belong. Take it. Go. Never come back! Never!"

That was all Michael needed to hear. "Thank you, sir. Thank you."

Michael bowed in submission, and with respect, as he backed away from the native man, away from the bonfire, and away from the bodies impaled around the fire.

Without another word, the young native led Michael and the others back toward the small river they had zip lined across . . .

Could they really be headed home?

# # #

The guide hopped on rocks crossing the stream. That was what it was now. A wide stream. The raging water had stopped. The flash flood, over. When he was on the other bank, he waved them over.

Michael looked at the others. Even if they fell off one of the rocks placed across the stream, they should be fine. The current seemed non-existent now.

Michael went first, holding the treasure chest like a running back would a football. It was cradled in his arms. He leapt from rock to rock without incident. When he made the last jump to the embankment, his heart almost stopped when the young native came at him.

The native caught his arm, and helped him finish the crossing without getting wet. Michael set the chest down, and encouragingly guided the others across.

They were not going to zip line back up the embankment. The guide knew a better, easier way. They had to follow him a quarter of a mile north. It was an ascent up the embankment, but climbable.

When they reached the rope extension bridge, Michael looked at Amber.

She shook her head.

Like Natalie, Amber seemed to have conquered her fears. Facing them head-on made a difference, he supposed. Amber went across the bridge first . . . She walked with purpose, with confidence, and without ever looking back.

The nights on the journey back to the boat were horrible. They didn't have tenting gear any longer. The bugs knew it, sensed a feast, and made no bones about sucking blood from weary Americans. The young guide slept soundly, as if the insects knew he was a native and simply left him alone.

They didn't sleep long, though. The young native took essentially catnaps. Then he would kick Michael awake. They hiked the trails all day, and most of the night. It seemed easier going on the way back. Maybe because the machetes had already cut a clean path. Maybe because they were over-tired, nearly delirious, and definitely suffering from some form of Post Traumatic Stress Disorder.

Before long, they'd reached the edge of the rainforest.

The young guide stopped and pointed.

Michael squinted as he peered into the distance.

"The boat," Tymere said.

Seas the Day. It was a sight for sore, sore eyes.

The native guide urged them forward, without taking another step himself.

Michael and the others thanked the young man, profusely. They watched the guide disappear back into the thick of the Amazon, before they turned and then broke into a run.

That boat represented many things to each of them. The boat meant they were alive. It meant they were free. It meant they escaped the jungle!

Once on the boat, with the engines running, and as they made their way back up the Xingu River, Marshall took a seat. He propped his elbows on his knees and buried his face in his hands.

Michael sat next to his friend. "You okay?"

Marshall didn't hide his tears. "For a minute there . . ."

Michael clapped him on the back. "Yeah, I know, buddy. I know."

After they put some distance between where they had docked, and where they were headed, Michael and the others gathered in the wheelhouse, at the helm. He set the small treasure chest on the table usually reserved for charting maps.

Everyone looked around at each other. Even Rosemary seemed transfixed on the idea of opening the wooden box.

With a pair of needle nose pliers and a thin screwdriver, Michael worked the old, rusty lock. He didn't want to break the box open. The chest itself could be quite valuable.

It didn't take much tweaking before the lock clicked open. Michael gripped the bulky lock in his hand, but stopped before he removed it from the latch.

"Before we open this, there are some things we need to talk about," Michael said.

Marshall sighed. "Are you serious? Open the chest."

"I'm being serious. Listen, there are all kinds of laws around finding treasure. For example, if we found this in New York, there is kind of a Finders Keepers law that would protect us, and we could keep whatever is inside," he explained.

"But we're not in New York," Marshall pointed out. "I know, Captain Obvious."

"That's true, though. We're not."

"We're from New York," Tymere said.

"I don't think that's going to matter," Rosemary added.

"What are the laws in Brazil? I mean, that's where we found the treasure." Amber folded her arms.

The bright sun came in through the wheelhouse windows. Outside, the sky was as blue as a robin's egg.

"The laws are all over the place. However, most indicate any dig that uncovers something of value, it belongs to the state. The government," Michael explained.

"Figures," Tymere said.

"The right thing to do is turn this chest over to the government, and hope we receive some kind of reward for the find," Michael said.

"Won't they want to know where we found the treasure?" Amber asked.

Rosemary said, "Then we would have to tell them about the temple, and natives."

"You're both right. That could really complicate things."

"Especially for the natives," Rosemary said. "The last thing those people need is an entire archaeological team plowing into their villages. Cutting down their trees. Excavating the tomb, again. They don't deserve that."

"I agree. I don't want to see that happen," Tymere said. "What are our other options?"

"We bring this home. Let me work with some of my father's old contacts. Talk with the family attorney, and see if we can find a reasonable, yet still diplomatic, way of getting rich without looking like tomb raiders. The thing is," Michael said, "we all need to agree on a path forward here."

"Even me?" Rosemary asked.

"Even you," Michael said.

"Let's see what's inside first," Natalie said.

"I think it is better we make a decision before we look inside. One we agree on, so that, no matter what we find, it won't influence us one way or the other. You know what I mean?" Michael said.

"I get it." Tymere nodded. "We commit first. Then we see."

"Right." Michael looked at his friends. "We have a few options. One, we turn this over to the Brazilian government as soon as we're . . . rescued, and hope there is some kind of reward or something for our efforts. Two, we bring it home and give it to a United States museum, with minimal explanation, let them deal with Brazil, and still hope there is a reward. Or three, like I said, when we get home, let me consult some of my father's contacts and stuff, and see what other options we might have. It might end up being the same two options, but at least we will have some more knowledgeable people helping us make the right choice."

"Three." Marshall nodded.

"Yeah, I'm going to side with Captain Obvious," Tymere said. "Three."

The ladies all agreed, as well.

Michael cleared his throat. "Three it is."

He stared down at the opened lock in his hand. "We ready?"

"Ready yesterday," Marshall said.

Michael removed the block from the latch. He gently set it aside. Slowly, he lifted the lid of the chest.

"Holy cow," Marshall gasped.

Inside the chest were hundreds of odd-shaped gold coins. Michael did not recognize the markings. "They're solid gold?"

Marshall fished one out and bit down on the piece. "They always do that in movies."

"And?" Natalie asked.

Marshall shrugged. "Have absolutely no idea what it is supposed to tell me."

Rosemary picked one up and turned it over in her hands for closer inspection. "It appears to be Italian. If I am not mistaken, it was issued by the Italian States in the early sixteen-hundreds. Sixteen hundred to sixteen twenty-two? They are known as the Two Doppie. The currency was known as the Lira. I only say that because, look here. There is the bust of a leader, and the writing is Italian. It reads - R-A-N-V-T F-A-R P-L-A P D-V-X I-V S R E C-O-N-F P-E-R."

"What does that mean?" Amber asked.

"I'm not certain." She looked at the back of the coin. "But with the wolf facing left, and the three-stemmed crown? I am almost positive that is what we have here."

Michael asked the question on everyone's mind. "What is a coin like that worth?"

Rosemary shook her head. "I am no numismatologist, but—"

"A what?" Marshall asked.

"Someone who studies and collects coins," Tymere explained.

"Right," Rosemary said. "I'm not one, but I would guess the coins are worth around three thousand dollars."

Michael felt deflated. After everything that happened, the booty was only $3,000. "Oh," he said.

"Apiece," Rosemary added.

"Apiece?" Natalie said, eyes wide. "There must be hundreds of coins in there."

11

September 15 - Rochester, NY

Michael Albright sat in his father's study. His textbooks for the new semester were stacked on a corner of the large mahogany desk. He leaned back in the large leather chair and finished reading an article about the death of the curator, Nicholas Katic.

The journalist covering the story, clearly, worked with what few facts were generally known by the public. The piece explained how Katic embarked on an unsanctioned, solo mission into the Amazon, searching for treasure to procure on behalf of the New York State Museum. The story indicated communication efforts were lost nearly a week after Katic's departure, that the Brazilian government was notified, and a two-week search for Nicholas Katic ensued. The map in the paper was of the northern Amazon Rainforest, along the Columbian borders. This was nowhere near where Katic actually died.

Michael supposed Rosemary fed skewed details to the authorities, ensuring the truth remained buried. Why? He wasn't exactly sure.

When his doorbell rang, Michael shot up from behind the desk. He practically ran through his house to the front door.

When everyone arrived, he had them sit in the dining room, just as he had done a few months ago, at the beginning of June.

"This is so oddly I, Michael," Amber announced.

"So much more so than you might realize."

"Oh, really?" Natalie asked.

Michael stood at the head of the table. The others, seated, watched him expectantly.

After several moments of silence, Marshall threw up his hands. "Well? Are you going to tell us what's going on, or are we supposed to guess?"

"I dropped out of school." Michael raised his eyebrows and didn't even try shielding his grin.

Amber stood up. "What? You did what? It's our senior year, Mike. We graduate this summer."

"Graduate with what?" Michael asked. "A b'chelor's degree in l–beral - nothing?"

"It's better than no degree at all," Natalie said.

"But is it?" Michael sat down next to Amber. "The Italian coins went on silent auction last week."

Everyone fell silent. The unanimous decision they agreed on was to sell the coins to a private collector. They rationalized away any guilt. The treasure was not necessarily Brazilian property. The chest wasn't mined, or unearthed on Brazilian land. Therefore, it wasn't technically something they felt should be returned to the Brazilian government.

Was it a loophole? Not really, Michael argued back, when they voted on what to do with the gold.

"And?" Natalie asked.

"It fetched over two point five million," he said.

"Holy cow," Marshall said.

"We owed fees to the auctioneer, and the lawyer, mind you," Michael said, "depending on how much you each decide to claim on your taxes . . ."

"Mike, c'mon, man!" Tymere looked ready to jump out of his seat. "What are we looking at?"

"Just about four hundred thousand each," Michael said.

Tymere fell back into his chair. His arms went limp at his sides. His dark skin looked pale, almost ghost-white.

"You okay?" Michael asked, laughing.

"You said each. We each get four hundred thousand?" Natalie asked.

"We do." Michael stood up again. "But that's not why I brought you all here tonight. Although, giving everyone a huge paycheck is a very good reason."

"Paycheck?" Amber asked.

"Paycheck. You see, it's why I am dropping out of school," he said.

"Mike, four hundred thousand dollars isn't going to last you a lifetime," Amber said. "I mean, I know your father left you the house and a pretty good-sized nest egg, but—"

"Amber, he left me more than that! He left me an office filled with his journals, and maps. He had charted out another thirty, forty expeditions, but never went on them," Michael explained. "I want to start a company with all of you—"

"I'm in," Marshall slapped his hands on the table.

"I didn't even say what it is yet," Michael said.

"Wait," Amber tried.

"I started a corporation. An archaeological company. We're going to go legit, and find more buried treasures. I have all the paperwork ready to go. We will be equal owners. We can—"

Amber stood up. "Mike, I'm going to medical school next fall. I have always dreamed of becoming a doctor. I'm so close to achieving my dream."

"But, Amber—"

"This isn't for me. What we survived is not for me. It's not my dream," she said.

"I'm in," Marshall said.

"Hold on, Marsh," Michael said. "Amber, let me finish, okay? Just, keep an open mind until I'm done?"

"You said equal owners?" Marshall asked. "I'm in."

Amber sat back down.

"Give me a second, Marsh." Michael cleared his throat. "Actually, I pretty much said everything there is to say."

"Can I document things?" Marshall asked. "I can vlog our expeditions, run our social media pages. Create our website."

"You absolutely can," Michael said. "That is exactly what I was hoping you'd volunteer to take charge of!"

"Wait until you see the compiled footage from the Amazon," Marshall said.

"I can't wait. When will it be ready?"

"Soon. Very, very soon," Marshall said. "I'm in."

"The thing is, I don't want any specifics of our expeditions revealed until after we've found whatever it is that we're looking for. You can create intrigue and mystery, you know? But people can't know any of the specifics. Agreed?"

Marshall nodded his head vigorously. "Absolutely. Agreed! I'm so in."

"Natalie, with your IT background, I figure your research skills will be invaluable. As well as possibly getting access into sites we might not otherwise have access to. You know, in case there are pieces of information we need," Michael shrugged, sheepishly.

"Oh, legit, huh?" Amber asked.

"I'm not talking about breaking into the Department of Defense websites, or anything like that—"

"I could probably do that, though." Natalie held up a finger. "Just saying."

"Good to know."

Amber let out a gasp. "I don't like this."

"And me?" Tymere asked.

"Like Amber, I know you have your eyes on law school. You have an archaeological background. Might be amateur level, but it is more than any of us have," Michael pointed out. "What do you think?"

Natalie didn't wait to be asked. "I'm in."

Michael stood up taller. "Okay. Marshall. Natalie. Awesome. Ty?"

He nodded his head. Slowly at first. Then he placed both his hands on the table. "Yeah. I'm in. In fact, I have been dying to take some archaeology classes. And there are a few history books I put off buying because of school. . ."

Amber stood up again. "Guys, I don't believe this. We're seniors. We are a heartbeat away from graduating."

"No one else has to quit school. You guys can probably take most of your classes online if you wanted to. I want to run this business. I can't do that and go to school at the same time. I don't want to divide my efforts."

"I want to be a doctor, Michael. You've known that from the day we first met," Amber said.

"You saved lives on our expedition, Amber. We need you."

She looked around the room, shook her head, and moved away from the table. "I have to go."

"Amber!"

"I need some time to think about this." She held up a hand, silently telling Michael not to follow her. "Please. Just give me some time."

EPILOGUE

Michael sat behind the desk in the study. Slowly, he came around to considering it his study, and not his father's.

Open on the desk was his laptop.

Marshall sent him a link to a YouTube video. The uploaded video hadn't been published on the site yet. Marshall was awaiting Michael's final approval.

The footage was less than optimal. Most of the dialogue was muffled, inaudible. That was Hanson's fault. Really, it was Michael's. He allowed Hanson to run the show.

He understood now why Hanson didn't want anything captured on camera or video. Hanson knew all along he intended on robbing everyone. Proof of his thievery would have been incriminating.

The video clarity was almost as bad as the audio.

The murder of Nicholas Katic was clear enough, though.

Michael paused the video.

He didn't need to rewatch the man getting gunned down in the small chamber inside the temple.

Michael switched to the email from Marshall and hit Reply.

I say we scrap this video, Michael typed out. Destroy it, even. We will start fresh with better cameras and sound mikes on our next adventure. Okay???

He closed the lid of his laptop as the doorbell rang.

Michael looked at his watch. It was only eight in the morning, and he wasn't expecting any company.

It had been a few days since his meeting with everyone, and he still hadn't heard from Amber. He understood her position. The idea of running this company without her bothered him.

He had no intentions of giving up on it, though. And, like Tymere, he was anxious to begin studying all things history. He had never felt so excited about learning before. Who would have guessed his father's passion would become his own?

Making his way around the desk, he also considered

working on learning new languages. He took a few years of Spanish in high school and college, but never applied himself. Maybe he could dig out his old textbooks and begin there?

Unlocking and opening the door, Michael took a step back.

Rosemary Katic stood on his front step.

"Ms. Katic."

"Mr. Albright."

"What can I do for you? Did you get the wire transfer?" Untraceable accounts had been created in foreign banks where the money from the sale of the coins had been deposited.

"I received the money, but that's not why I'm here."

He stepped aside, letting Rosemary into the house. "Something to drink?"

"Yes. Please."

"Wine? Beer? Something stronger?"

She arched an eyebrow. "I was thinking . . . coffee?"

"Coffee. Right. Come in. Have a seat." He indicated the barstool by the breakfast nook while he removed two cups from the cupboard.

"If you have any Baileys?" she added.

"I think we can accommodate you there," he said, grinning.

"The reason I'm here . . . I understand you and your friends started a new business together. A treasure hunting company."

Michael wasn't sure how word would have gotten out. The corporate name was simple, Albright & Albright. There were no specifics listed that would have revealed the nature of the venture. The lawyer helped craft everything carefully for that reason. Secrecy.

"I'm not sure . . ."

She waved a dismissive hand. "I want in."

"In?"

"I want to work for you. I will take my bar exam in two months. I can be your in-house attorney," she offered.

"In-house attorney?"

"And I want to go on expeditions with your team," she said.

Ah, he thought. Now we're getting to the meat of the matter. "Ms. Kati—"

"Rosemary, please."

"Rosemary, I—"

She pulled something out of her purse and slapped it down

on the counter.

"What is that?"

"Something my father was working on," she said.

"Is that what I think it is?" Michael asked, the bottle of Baileys in his hand forgotten.

"It is. It's a map to a long lost treasure . . ."

THE END

AUTHOR'S NOTE

Writing an action / adventure book on travel is no simple feat. It takes a ton of research. While this is a fiction novel, so many of the details needed to be based on facts. I did a considerable amount of research on Brazil, and the Amazon Rainforest. I looked at the terrain, animals, insects, and weather. I learned about the vegetation, the rivers, and the natives.

There was a pirate named "Roche Braziliano." Although, his real name was more than likely, Gerrit Gerritszoon. He was born in the small Dutch town of Groningen in 1630 and disappeared in 1671, at the age of 41. Author Alexandre Equemelin made the pirate famous in his book *The Buccaneers of America*. He was a privateer in Brazil until around 1954, when he moved to Jamaica and became a notorious pirate of the Caribbean. He roasted alive two farmers on spits when they refused to give him their pigs. He was known to cut off the limbs of Spanish prisoners before roasting them alive, as well.

In 1671 he vanished. Possibly he and his crew were lost at sea, or captured by the Spanish. No one knows for sure.

It is important to note any inaccurate historical information, or details about Brazil, or the Amazon was done to ensure the way I wanted the story of *Temple of Shadow* told. I took plenty of liberties, and admit it openly. Hopefully readers can look past factual errors and enjoy the tale I've spun.

As always, thank you for your support!

PT3
12/2021

ABOUT THE AUTHOR

Phillip Tomasso is an award-winning author of numerous novels and short stories. He works full time as a Fire/EMS Dispatcher for 911. As a father of three, he spends any spare time with his family, writing and playing guitar. He is hard at work on his next novel.

SPECIAL THANKS

No book writes itself. I have so many people to thank. I hope I do not leave anyone out. First, to my Beta Readers: Katie Kast, Morgan Gleisle, and Lisa Rice. To my personal editor and friend, Tamra Crow. My editor at Severed Press, Nichola Meaburn, gave the manuscript a very good once-over, or twice-over. Somehow I spelled Michael wrong more than half the time! (Regardless of editing countless passes, any mistakes still found within the pages are solely mine). Lastly, I would like to thank Gary Lucas and the entire Severed Press staff for their continued support, encouragement and tireless efforts to sell books!

Made in United States
North Haven, CT
26 April 2022

18574463R00117